Red Dragon Square

by

Yvonne Wilson

DREAMCATCHER PUBLISHING
Saint John ◆ New Brunswick ◆ Canada

Canadian Cataloguing in Publication Data

Yvonne Wilson - 1927

Red Dragon Square

Fiction - Spirtual Journey - Literary Fiction

ISBN - 1-894372-03-4

Editor: Patricia Blackman

Cover Photo and Design: Ken Spink of Inspiration Graphics

Background Photo - Freeman Patterson

Young Men on front Cover - Scott Mitchell right - Jamie Margaris - left

Printed and bound in Canada: Unipress Ltd.

DREAMCATCHER PUBLISHING INC.
1 Market Square
Suite 306 Dockside
Saint John, New Brunswick Canada E2L 4Z6
www.dreamcatcher.nb.ca

For Kate and Lucy

Acknowledgements

Red Dragon Square is the culmination of many years of living and learning, and for it I must thank everyone I ever met, every place I ever knew, and all the people who ever taught me or allowed me to teach them. They are all part of the experience that went into this story.

I want to single out two special friends: Patricia Blackman, my editor and staunch supporter, and Elizabeth Margaris, my publisher, without whom it is not a polite formula to say that this book would never have been between covers.

I also want to record my delight in the cover of this book. To Freeman Patterson, for allowing us to use his magnificent photo of the Andes as a background, and to Ken Spink (Inspiration Graphics) for the design, many thanks.

Yvonne Wilson

Red Dragon Square is a vortex into which humanity sweeps, and swirls round and round. Mountain people wash up there. Old families break away and disappear down the delta. Everyone is on the move, but nobody goes back to the mountains - nobody but "two crazymen striding north" while "tired-looking men with heavy packs and women carrying children" hurry south. Arnolds says, "They'd turn when they left us behind...and we'd wave to them."

Other Works by Yvonne Wilson

Fiction:

Slipper Hbr.-a novel for children

Edited Fiction:

Dublin: Daughter of Merchant Kings by P.D. Whelan
Overtime by Brad Janes
Fritz of Arnhem (Cdn. & U.S. editions) by Edis A. Flewwelling

Edited Non-fiction:

Traffic Crash Analysis: Court Preparation Manual by Thomas Watters
Tales of Lonewater Farm by Edis A. Flewwelling
Victim to Victory by Lynn Freeze
I Count Only the Sunny Hours: Memories of an Army Wife by Simone Walker

Edited: Self-help:

Be Who You Are With Love: A Spiritual Journey by Catherine Doucette

Edited: Poetry

Tomorrow's World by Richard Doiron

Red Dragon Square

Part 1

"... thorns shall come up in her palaces,
nettles and brambles in the fortresses thereof:
and it shall be an habitation of dragons,
and a court for owls."

(Isaiah 34:13)

Chapter: 1

The Red Dragon was warming but still only stirring in his sleep when the local bus drew up at the mouth of the Square and dropped me off to walk the rest of the way home.

Three years since I'd seen the Square. I'd have known where I was, though, if I'd been coming in from outer space. I mean, just like they always were, the night shutters were dragged across the arcade arches and held in place with padlocks and rusty chains; but the mouse-holes, that I used to come and go by when I was a mouse growing up under the dragon's eye, were still there, if you knew where to look for them. And Creaky Fred, Red Andy's head waiter— "Creaky" because he had a stiff knee— was on the sidewalk under the awning, shaking out tablecloths, and making sure no early mouse came too close to the rolls or ran a grubby hand along a chair back.

I walked right past Red Andy's and wished old Creaky good-morning, but he didn't know me. Maybe it was the pack on my shoulder. Never mind. My sister might not know me either, after three years and the night bus from Hawberry.

In the slip at the far end of the Square, seven or eight black canal barges were lined up gunwale to gunwale. Most of them were quiet, but two were working, even just after sunrise, and I walked all the way down and stood watching a cargo-sling lifting wicker baskets onto the pier. Or maybe I stopped for a few deep breaths before starting up the alley and facing Ern.

Those few deep breaths, even if I'd been a blindman, would have told me the Square wasn't quite the same as I left it— Luigi's Fish and Chips was gone. Well, Ern would be pleased. But I felt a little disappointed. Must have been looking forward to strolling down to the cart for a paper of spuds and mudshark. Practically grew up on Luigi's fish and chips.

But... A few deep breaths and Luigi was gone, and I'd have to get used to the new, worse smell that was hanging around in his place.

By this time, though, I was crossing the Square, coming back from the slip on an angle, and I forgot the messages my nose was sending because I was looking at this pile of folded and corded packing material leaning against the alley-wall of the General Outfitters and extending inwards as far as I could see. At first I thought the alley was blocked off altogether, but a passage just wide enough for a man to sidle through was left on the warehouse side.

Now that took me back a bit!— back to when nothing kept the alley mice of my day out so late, or made the time so short, as a pile of dry cardboard cartons against the General Outfitters' wall...

Especially me and Ben Fagan.

Especially me and Ben because most mice had mouse-mothers, and mouse-mothers had voices that could slither through any wall or slide under any fence, without half trying. But Ben had only his father, who worked evenings. And Ern's voice... Well, I didn't always hear Ern's voice back then.

Usually the piles of boxes— what we didn't carry off— disappeared in a day or two. But a pile one summer lasted two weeks and three days, and I never had a better time. I wouldn't have gone home to bed at all if Ben would have stayed out with me. But every evening, the minute the bells started calling the monks to their last prayers for the day, he ran off.

After this happened a few times I started wondering why. Why would Ben be going home every night an hour or two before his old man would be looking for him? So I followed him. And what I saw nearly fried my brains.

Here's Ben— Ben Fagan, that wouldn't even go to the Evangelical Sunday School when there was something free being given out... Here's Ben sneaking into the back of the church!!

Sneaking in, and flopping on his knees. Kneeling! Ben Fagan! Right there in the back row. Down on his knees. Praying.

I hid in the porch and grabbed him when he came out. Grabbed him by the band of his shorts and twisted till his breath got shallow.

"What were you doing in there?" I hissed.

He tried to fend me off, but I gave him another twist.

"Let me go, Arnold," he gasped. "I can't breathe."

"What were you doing!"

"What did it look like!"

"What were you doing, Ben! Tell me and I'll quit twisting your pants."

"All right!.. I was praying."

"I could see that!" I yelled. "What for!?"

"Ssh-h! He'll hear you!" Ben whispered, and tried to drag me away into the garden.

"Aw, I'm not scared of no old monk," I hollered.

"Not them, Arnold," Ben says. "Him. You know." And he points upward.

"Oh, for God's sake!" I hooted.

"Arnold!" he screeched. "Shut up! Please! Shut up!"

By this time he has me dragged out through the garden gate and we're standing where the path to his alley starts squeezing between our house and the monastery wall. At least, I'm standing. Ben has calmed down some, but he's still dancing around like a bee in a bottle.

"He'll hear you!" he's panting. "He does, you know. He hears me!"

"You mean He hears you?" I'm saying. "Up there?"

"Yes," he's telling me. "Yes. You gotta believe me, Arnold. I asked every night this week for the waste-paper barge to get stuck down the water. And it hasn't showed up yet!"

When he finished saying this he was already sliding toward the passage, moving fast.

I stood and watched him go. Thought of chasing the little bastard home, but Ern was leaning over the verandah railing, watching me...

So I was feeling about eleven or twelve coming up the alley. Not your ideal age for confronting Ern, seeing I was three years late. And there she was, on the verandah, watering a tub of pink geraniums.

"Been sleeping in your clothes?" she says.

"What happened to Luigi?" was what I said to her.

"Cops ran him off," she said. "Receiving sacks of acrite pods along with the spuds. Or so they say."

"I'm smelling something new," I said, "now that Luigi's gone. Or was it always there?"

Ern sniffed. "Oh, that! Bargeload of hides in the slip," she said. "Been there a day or two. You'll never notice once you clear the fresh air out of your nose... That is where you been, I suppose?"

I nodded.

"Cranky came back."

That was a surprise.

"Stays in your sleep-out," she told me. "I feed him and see he has water. Outside of that, Cranky and I don't see eye to eye."

No. They wouldn't. They never did. "But," I thought, "he's another reason I had to come back. Had to see to my crankybird before I could shake the dust of Red Dragon Square off my boots forever— along with Luigi, and the geraniums, and all the rest of it."

I turned toward my sleep-out still talking to Ern. "What's the matter?" I said. "You should be getting ready for work this time of day. Laid off or something?"

"Promoted!" she says. "Supervisor on the swing shift! Get you a job if you like."

"What! Unloading barges?"

"Oh-h!" she says. "Above the canal now, are we?"

I didn't answer. What I said was, "Aw, Ern!" And she knew I wasn't talking about the canal but about what I was seeing through the sleep-out door.

"Well, how was I to know!" she starts in. "You could've been dead and buried. Never a word from one year's end to the next..."

"I know. I know," I said, because I didn't want to get into that. "You don't need to remind me... Is there any lemon jilly in the house?"

"I think so," she said.

"Then bring out a jug and a couple of glasses," I told her. "We can sit under the tree till I recover from the shock and work up the strength..."

She looked like she could say a lot if she liked but decided to bite her tongue and go in the house instead. And I sprawled in an old canvas deck chair under the flame tree, and heard it all anyway.

"Arnold," she would have started in, "you should be grateful you have a good home to come to." I was. I just wasn't there.

She would have pointed out that a nicer house than ours couldn't be found in Red Dragon Square. I might have pointed out to her that all we had of the house was three rooms on the ground floor and the same above— on the back of the building, mind you! And a sleep-out added on later, when they needed a coal hole. But I wouldn't have said a word. It was Ern's house, and she was proud of it.

Once she got started she would have told me to remember we actually owned this house. And garden! No rent to pay like everybody else she knew. I might have reminded her that taxes come pretty high in the City. But Ern paid the taxes.

She would certainly have made me remember we owned— actually owned— the ground we were standing on, because our family owned it going back to the Dark Ages. How many people could say that?! And I wouldn't have said a word about the land we were standing on being barely enough for me to get my feet on, both at once.

She would have had something to say about the tree. Nobody but us, for miles around, had a tree that grew right out of the ground, not out of a tub— except the monks.

And before she finished, she wouldn't have missed the point that I never used the place anyway, except to keep my stuff in, including that dirty crankybird! So which leg did I have to stand on, please?

Cranky swooped down and perched on the top of the tree. It being wintertime, the branches were bare and the tree looked dead. Against Cranky's bright blue feathers it looked like it died a long time ago. For a minute I had this sinking feeling it did and I ought to get out of there before Ern found out and went into deep mourning. But she'd have noticed the tree. Looked after it like it was a plaster saint in a niche.

Oh, yes. She would've seen the tree. Probably never saw the warehouse wall, though, which looked to me like she would, one of these days, when it came down on her begonias.

And there was the upstairs flat. She must know that was empty. No baby carriages. No bicycles. No curtains in the windows. Wondered about that. Ern never had trouble finding tenants.

After that, to give myself a little space, I glanced toward the monastery garden. The monks never shut the gate and we could always... see... right across...

"Ern!" I hollered. "The gate's shut!"

"I know," she hollered back through the kitchen window. "They had to close the garden. Too many bums. But I have a key. Show you the azaleas later."

All of a sudden a red splotch fell on my shoulder. For a minute I thought it was a petal off the tree; but when I reached up to take it in my hand, it was wet— a red, wet petal off a winter flame tree; a wet, red petal with a blue sheen.

I held it on the tip of my finger. I knew it was a bloodied bit of feather. Had to be.

Then another piece fell.

"Come on down, Cranky," I called then, softly. "Somebody hurt you, baby? Somebody taking pot shots at my boy, are they? Never mind, fellah, you'll be all right. You and me'll clear out of Red Dragon Square in a day or two. Come on down. Come, birdie!"

But he wouldn't come. Didn't remember me yet, I guess. And when Ern came out with a tray in both hands and the screen door slammed, he squawked and took off just like the day I thought I lost him for good...

Everything, that day in the barge under the kiri trees, was in deep shadow, all but the wicker cage under the hatch, where light poured straight in. Two birds were dead already, and Cranky was standing over the third with his wings half raised and his beak open. Nobody moved. Nobody made a sound. And Johnny's arm shot up and the top of the cage splintered.

One smooth motion. Johnny's bare arm flashes. The cage is a bunch of twigs showering down. And Cranky lifts against the sun till he's only a long, thin wail.

We left before the crowd was sure what happened!

"Why in hell did you do that?!" I yell, as we're making tracks for the bridge and the lot where we left Johnny's car.

"Thought I would," he says...

Cranky looked all right as he flew, but I'd have to get him away soon, before somebody made a trophy of him.

Ern and I watched him go. Then we settled down in the alley and spent the rest of the day under the tree, with the Square humming behind us and the canal steaming a faint odor of oil and hot, raw hides. I soon got used to it and hardly noticed.

Gradually familiar things, familiar ways oozed back into me and I lost the feeling I was a stranger sitting there. Every time I moved, my chair split a little down the back, but I wasn't surprised and it didn't bother me. Ern's chair wobbled every time she reached for her drink, as I knew it would. But I also knew it wouldn't tip her over. Our old chairs were like our old tree, always had one more spring in them. And that was the way things were in Red Dragon Square.

"So where's Johnny?" Ern says, when it began to get dark and she started feeling hungry. "About time for supper, about time for Johnny."

"Johnny's not here," I said. "He didn't come."

"He didn't come!" she hollers. "Don't tell me you came home without him!"

"What's the matter with you?" I said. "I thought you didn't like Johnny."

"I got nothing against Johnny," she says, still hollering. "Except he's a bad influence. It's his mother!"

"What about his mother!?"

"She's a pain in the..."

"Miz Doyle?" I croaked. "What are you talking about!? You don't know Miz Doyle!"

"That's all you know," she says. "Su and Ern are pals now. Bosom buddies!"

"What!?"

"Oh, yes! Rings me up all the time, Su does. Usually when I'm just coming in from work and all I want is a shower and a cold drink. But that's Su!"

"What does she want!?"

"What does she want!" Ern echoed. "There's only one thing Su Doyle wants. She wants that precious son of hers."

"But..."

"She thinks I hear from you."

"But..."

"Well, it would be natural."

"Yes, but..."

"So she rings me up. I say, 'No, Miz Doyle, no word yet.' She thanks me like I did her some great favour. And seventy-four and a half minutes later, by my watch, she's at the door with a big smile on."

I sat up so fast the back of my chair parted another six or seven inches. "Su Doyle comes here!?" I yelled.

"That's what I'm telling you," Ern says. "In the neighbourhood, you know. Couldn't pass me by!"

"But..."

"Not sure she can believe what I tell her over the phone, of course, and thinks I can't see through her."

"But..." I tried to get words out but I never got farther than sputtering.

"Can't you see Su Doyle shopping Red Dragon Square? Getting her hair done at Minnie's? Taking tea at Henry's deli?"

No, I couldn't see it. No more could anybody else.

"The first few times," Ern said, "I listened to her till I thought I'd die of starvation. After that I got smart. 'Miz Doyle,' I said, 'have you dined? There's nothing in the house. But Archie's Bar and Grill in the East Arcade does a nice steak.' So now we eat out."

She giggled and slapped my arm. "Archie and me are getting to be just like that," she says. "Wonder what he'd say if he knew who my girlfriend really was."

"Archie Mundy?" I scoffed. "He wouldn't know Su Doyle if you hit him over the head with her. Miz Doyle goes there!?"

"Never notices a thing," Ern said. "Long's I'll listen to her talking about Johnny. Where is he, anyway? She'll never let me rest if she finds out you're here and he's not."

"Johnny's up to Medalsring," I said.

Ern's eyes flew open. "Medalsring?" she gasped. "You mean..? Dead?"

"No, no," I said. "That's just an old story. Medalsring's not... that. It's a real place. Meadows of Perpetual Spring. I just came back from there. But Johnny stayed."

Ern looked at me like she never saw me before. Then she reached out cautiously and pinched my arm. Solid enough!

After that we sat in the dusk for a few minutes, not talking. Me thinking of the place in the mountains, Medalsring, where I left Johnny. Ern, I guess, deciding whether to believe me or not to. After awhile she must've made up her mind, because she started with the questions.

"Medalsring is away to hell and gone," I told her. "Well, no, put it the other way around. Medalsring is pretty close to heaven. Not heaven itself, but close— way up in the high country, above the swirling water: space, Ern; fresh air; room for the wind to blow and the rain to fall; snow, too... You maybe wouldn't like it, but it suits me down to the ground. I'll be going back there in a few days."

At that she drew in her breath pretty sharp.

"Isn't that just like you, Arnold Grieve," she snapped. "Home five minutes and can't wait to be on the road again. After I haven't seen you for over three years and more. What's to become of you? Aren't you ever going to settle down? It was bad enough when you went away up to Wooji..."

"Oh, we been away beyond Wooji this time," I told her. "Wooji's just down the corner of the Square compared to where we been."

Ern shuddered. She was funny that way. Spent all her life right there in the Square. Worked around the canal since she was fifteen. Married a bargee, briefly. And never had a dream beyond owning a flower stall in the South Arcade.

Once when we were kids we went down the water for a day with a bargee we knew. Went right up to Commercial Square that was just finishing being built then. Ern held my hand the whole way— trying to make out she was taking care of me!

After we got to the Square she was all right as long as we stayed on the ground spending money in the stalls. But one of the buildings had a glass elevator up the outside, and I was bound and determined to get in.

Ern tried to talk me out of it, but when she saw she couldn't she got in with me, hanging onto my hand and keeping her eyes screwed tight.

It was great. I had the time of my life— till Ern accidentally opened her eyes a slit and all hell broke loose! One look out over the miles and miles of City down below and she near tore the cage out by the roots trying to get off. Wouldn't go more than two blocks from home for years after.

While I was remembering that and laughing to myself, Ern must've been trying to picture Wooji, which she thought was about at the end of the world. I guess she was doing that, because all of a sudden she giggled and said, "That's how I handle my pal Su."

"What do you mean?" I asked, dragging my mind back.

"Wooji," she hooted, like she sneaked up behind somebody and said 'Boo!' "Su hates the place. She thinks you and Johnny love it."

"We did," I said, "but we finished with it. Seam ran out."

I didn't mean gold, but I didn't want to get into what I did mean, so I let it go at that.

Johnny and me were mining up the South Flank out of Wooji when we met. Couldn't stand him at first. Hand-sewn boots. Hand-sewn wallet full of credits. Big blue eyes. Thick black curls. Thought he wouldn't last to the next haircut.

Last! Johnny settled in like he was born on the place. Nobody worked harder. Nobody laughed easier. And nobody fought dirtier, when required. It was Johnny took me over, not the other way around. I didn't start looking after him till a lot later... Not till after Jenny.

I shook my head. "Poor old Johnny," I said.

"Poor Johnny my foot!" Ern says. "Don't forget I know all about him. Talk about your silver spoons!"

"That's just it," I said. "So many silver spoons he was near choked to death. Just as fast as he'd spit one out, Su'd shove another one in. But up to Wooji he only had two or three left, and he was so used to them he never noticed... Till Jenny..."

"Till Jenny," Ern said, kind of quiet. "Always we come back to Jenny. According to Su, Johnny was your perfect little poppet, till he met Jenny. According to you, Johnny was the best mate in the world, till he met Jenny. What was this Jenny anyway? Angel or something?"

"Johnny thought she was."

"And you didn't?"

"No, I probably did too. She was pretty enough to be one. Great big dark eyes. Long straight hair. Walked nice. But the angel Johnny saw was inside her."

I stopped. It doesn't come easy to me to talk about feelings. But Ern knew that and fed me easy questions till I started telling her the whole story. Night was coming on and we hadn't had a bite to eat since morning, but still we sat there talking.

"When we were up to Wooji," I said, "we worked for this mining company that was dredging for alluvial gold."

Ern probably didn't understand more than a tenth of what I told her about the big dredges, the water pressure that we had, or didn't have. About stuff flowing down the flume we built. And about working sun-up to sun-down ten days at a time and it hot enough to burn the paint right off a peaked tin roof, without the word of a lie.

She didn't follow much, but she didn't make a sound either till I got to the part about the four days off we had after the ten days on. "Ah-h," she said then, like we were finally coming to the good part.

"Pay was good," I said. "So after work we got cleaned up and went to town."

Not that there was much to Wooji itself. Your standard mining town— one pub for every two houses and them all squat and dust-coloured. Tin rooves. Deep verandas. Flimsy construction. Hard-packed earth instead of paving. Cactus and salt bush for flowers. Trees here and there— growing in the ground, of course. And outside plumbing, mostly. Pretty standard. Flat. Laid on a dry lake bed, this being desert country and hot. At the back, this old slime dump everybody called "the rise." And in the distance, these low hills where the gold was supposed to be.

Johnny kept a room at the Union Hotel. All the time. To keep his clean shirts and that in. Worked great for awhile. Nobody more popular at the Union than Johnny and me. Till one night a truckload of goons from a company sluicing the North Flank came in and took over the bar.

I grinned, remembering, and my tongue ran over the caps on three of my front teeth...

They had this grand staircase at the Union. White-painted ironwork. Red carpet. Wide enough for six guys abreast. And curving, nice and slow. Only thing was, anybody looking out of the bar could see anybody on the stairs.

So here comes Johnny down the staircase. White silk slacks, like he was poured into them. Handmade white shoes. White shirt with a frill down the front. This black wool jacket with real gold buttons. And him fresh from the barber, every curl polished!

Wooji never saw anything like him! I laugh every time I think of it. Manager didn't though.

Johnny paid for the damage, of course, and let the old crook skin him for twice what we really did. But we had to find another place to stay after that. By the next day our names were mud and nobody would have us inside of two miles of any place. So we ended up buying a shack across the rise, out on the edge of the bush. Well, I say "we." Johnny bought it. I never had money for buying shacks and that.

First thing he did... First thing he did, he found this can of paint and painted "Home Sweet Home" over the door. Then he put our names under it: "J. Doyle," "A. Grieve". And "Friends Welcome." After that he just laid in a supply of beer and waited for the party to happen.

We didn't have to wait long, and it was a great party. But right after that... he met Jenny.

There was half a dozen shacks along our road. Most of them falling down. On the north we had this hill family— when they weren't gone walkabout. On the other side... Well, that was Jenny. And Johnny saw her first thing the first morning we woke up in our new house.

I should say Johnny woke up. I sort of came to with his hand slapping the window screen beside my head and his shadow falling across my bed. He was out on the verandah yelling stuff like "Come on, Arnold, roust yourself out of there, mate," and something about morning and the bowl of night.

"Go soak your head in the bowl of night," I told him, but he only laughed and kept slapping at the screen.

When I couldn't take much more of that, I staggered out of bed and out onto the verandah.

The sun wasn't even up yet, but Johnny was standing right where it was getting ready, and he looked like he was sparkling all over. I was so sure, I reached out and felt him. Then I realized he was wet, which cleared up the mystery— maybe.

We used to do that up to Wooji— stand under the shower, clothes and all, I mean. Only way to get cooled off some days. That was what Johnny did. Stood under the shower and never bothered with a towel. You could see his footprints in the dust on the verandah where he walked with wet feet. But when Johnny did things... Well, to be honest, sometimes it was hard to tell. He might've been just showering like anybody else. But then again, being Johnny, he might've been making rain, or collecting dew right out of the air. I always had the feeling I never knew.

Well, I mean I wasn't the only one watching him that morning, and we were all standing with our mouths open.

There was me, looking at where the sun was going to come up and seeing sparkles. There was this dirty half-grown kid peeking over the back fence and staring like he was seeing the Feather-foot or something.

And then there was Jenny. She was standing outside her back door in a loose white nightgown and her hair all wet and hanging down her back.

At first Johnny didn't know all this staring was going on and he started to say something. But he must've sensed the kid and Jenny because he swung round and looked at them.

Soon as he did that the kid disappeared, but Jenny never moved. I can see her to this day just like she was then. So can Johnny, I think, and I guess it's like having a bunch of hornets down your shirt— which happened to us one day. I mean, I saw her with my eyes all squinted up, half asleep, half hung-over. But Johnny saw her clear and clean, right through to the halo and the wings that he always swore were there.

Behind her you could see her garden, if you could call it that— three dry rose bushes trying to put out leaves, this little patch of burnt grass, and the biggest prickly pear I ever saw in my life. Back of that... Back of all of us... Just miles and miles of scrubby desert.

In the silence you could hear a little trickle of water running from a garden hose under the rose bushes.

Then, suddenly the sun came up, and it was like somebody dropped a match on a patch of gasoline.

I turned away and shut my eyes, so I didn't see what happened next. Heard it though. This screen door banged. This big dog burst out of Jenny's house, fast and growling. Jenny screamed. And somebody shot by me and into our house.

It happened so fast I was still spinning when Johnny pushed me through the door and we ended up looking at the kid crouched behind a chair in a corner of our kitchen.

Well, that was the poorest, dirtiest, scrawniest kid I ever saw. Dirt like you wouldn't believe. Ragged old orange sweater. One shoe on, one gone— lost coming up our steps. This old scrape on the left shin opened up again and bleeding into his sock. And the smell of him, sort of wafting through the house and starting out the windows. But when he dared to look up, he had these beautiful black eyes, and them about as scared as eyes can get.

I stood blinking, but Johnny gives me a shove toward the pantry. "Did we get any food in, Arnold?" he says.

I didn't think we did, but I rummaged around and found some bread and butter and tea. Johnny turned up a tin of jam out of another bag of stuff, which we opened with a screwdriver, not having a can opener.

And all the time the kid's watching us from the corner. He looked like he'd climb straight through the wall if we twitched, and I figured getting close to him would be like getting close to a cougar cub, but while the kettle was coming to the boil, Johnny jumped him and threw him in the shower.

He made some howls then! But he knew what to do, specially with us standing over him watching that he did it, and by the time he came out he was much improved, though he still looked scared into next week.

Johnny finished the treatment by plonking three mugs down on the table and pouring out the tea.

Well, I drank my share, but I couldn't eat. Half the time I couldn't keep my eyes open for the room spinning around. And I know Johnny didn't eat much. But the loaf of bread was almost gone by the time we all agreed we'd had our breakfast.

"What's your name?" Johnny says then.

"Egan."

"Egan, for God's sake!" I said. "Where'd you get a fancy name like that?"

"Dunno."

"Where do you live?"

He jerked a thumb over his shoulder. Could've been anywhere, but it turned out he was one of the clan that used the shack along the road.

"Do you go to school?"

"Dunno."

"Then I guess we'll drop you off there on our way," Johnny says.

At that point the kid tried to dodge between us, but we headed him off and pinned him in the old pickup we used to drive up there.

"Where's the school?" Johnny says.

"Dunno."

"Then we'll find it."

And that was how we saw Jenny the second time. While we watched to see that somebody got hold of Egan and marched him into school, this old sedan drove up and Jenny and this big, soft-looking, good-looking...

"Don't swear!" Ern barked— it was automatic with her.

"I'm not," I said. "Just running over a short description of our dear friend and neighbour Farmer Greene, Jenny's husband."

"Oh, no," Ern says. "I never heard she had a husband. Don't tell me she was married!"

I got up then and sauntered down the lane, and Ern followed. It was pitch dark under the flame tree by this time, and cooling off. Time to eat. We avoided Archie's. Probably scared Miz Doyle would find us there. Went to a new place in the East Arcade instead, where Ern said she heard the food was good.

Wasn't a bad place. Crowded. But it gave me this creepy feeling I'd been there before. Kept expecting somebody to come in that I knew up-country. And wouldn't you know? Just as we're coming out I squeeze by this big guy in the doorway and he yells after me, "Hey! Aren't you Arnold Grieve?"

I turned and looked at him and he was all smiles. "Yes, sir! It's Arnold Grieve," he hollers. "How ya been?"

"Great," I said, and gave him a big smile in return. Didn't know him from Adam.

Ern and I kept on heading out, but he pushes after us, grabs me by the hand and starts pumping. "Well, it's a small world," he hollers. "This the Missis?"

"My sister Erna," I said.

"Glad to meet you, Erna," he hoots. "Any sister of Arnold's! Me and him is old friends from up to Wooji there. Me and my mates was sluicing the North Flank when him and his mates was on the South. Never forget it as long as I live." Then he draps his arm around Ern's shoulders and gives her a squeeze like she might've got from a bull elephant. "Ern, honey," he says, "that brother of yours give me the finest evening I ever spent in all my life. Wish you could've seen it..! You wasn't there?"

"No," Ern says, sort of through her teeth. "No, I never been to Wooji."

"You'll love it," he tells her. "Great little town, Wooji. Stay at the Union!"

By that time I had a pretty good idea who he was, and I was about to try and get Ern away, when he gives me this dig in the ribs and says, "Best little bar on the fields, ain't that right, mate."

"Yes," I said. "Great place."

"They done it up, you know," he says to me, getting all confidential. "Never know the place. Even got a picture of our evening painted on the back wall. You're in it, and of course your mate there, Johnny, he's front and centre. You'll have to see it."

I laughed and he saw my teeth. "See you got fixed up all right," he says. "Done a real good job."

He took hold of my face and pulled my lip back so he could get a better look and I almost gave him the second greatest evening of his life right then and there, but I had Ern to think of. "Yes, sir, real good job," he says. "Never know they was ever broke, would you. Me now..."

He held up his left hand and showed us a scar across the knuckles.

"You lost your teeth, mate!" he hollers, "And I smashed up my left-hand knuckles! But they went for a good cause!"

Then he throws his arms around the both of us. "Look who's here!" he bellows.

"Damn! It's the Wooji Wonder!" somebody hollers, and half the goons in the arcade rush up and grab my hand.

Hours later we still had a hard time getting away from them. Only the fact Ern had to go to work saved us.

"Arnold," she started in as soon as we got clear. "Arnold, I don't believe it. Is that the kind of friends..."

"Friends!" I hooted. "They're my enemies!"

We laughed all the way home.

And after that, if I had to account for the rest of that night, I'd say I slept on Ern's new sofa in the front room. But I spent most of it either laughing or what you might call dreaming, of places way up-country where I'd been with Johnny.

I'd have to call his mother pretty soon.

Chapter: 2

Next day, as soon as daylight was strong enough, I put in a couple of hours cleaning the sleep-out. Then I went down the Square and bought paint and whitewash. While that dried, I moved down a mattress from the upstairs flat.

By that time the day was hot and so was I— hot enough to make the old chairs under the tree look pretty good. So I laid back and watched a big bird circling high in the air over the warehouse. Figured it was Cranky, but he didn't come down.

After awhile Ern came out in ironed jeans and a white shirt. Ern's a good-looking girl, little and fair, and I wondered why she didn't do something with her life instead of throwing it away on Red Dragon Square.

"Clean yourself up," she said, "and we'll get out of here before somebody comes and spoils the day."

I thought she was thinking of Miz Doyle. But it was a bald-headed guy went by, when we were sitting in Red Andy's eating hot squiggy buns, and made her lose the middle out of hers.

Ern and I been eating Andy's hot strawberry squiggy buns for as far back as I remember. I think of them all the time when I'm away, and I was just biting into my second one when Ern dives behind my shoulder.

"Don't look now," she hisses, "but is that bald-headed guy coming this way?"

I wasn't going to lose my strawberries so I took my time answering, but I lost them anyway because she gave me this ferocious jab in the ribs and hissed again, "Is he coming?"

"No," I said, as soon as I could talk for the pain in my fingers where the hot jam landed. "No, he's going down the Square."

She let out her breath. "Come on, then," she says, "we'll go the other way. But keep your eye out for bald heads."

"Why?"

"Never mind. I don't want to see that guy today, that's all."

"Coming on to you?" I suggested, with what I figured was a fine leer, but she only looked disgusted and dragged me out of Red Andy's and up the Square to Leona's where there was an empty table away at the back.

It was the hottest part of the day. I kicked my sandals off and rubbed my feet in the dust. And without any warning at all Red Dragon Square faded out and I was leaning on the bar in the Wooji Flanks Hotel watching Jenny do that selfsame thing, work her sandals off with her toes and dry her feet in the dust under the table.

It was a Friday and we just got into town. Funny how I saw it all so clear...

Johnny downed his first beer and passed back for a refill.

"Sizzling out on the flats today, Amy," he told the barmaid. "My veins feel all closed down for lack of moisture. That first drink is getting into some of them, but it's nowhere near enough."

"Seems cool in here," Amy said, "but I can tell it's hot in town. Look at that wilted bunch of teachers down the back if you don't believe me."

Johnny jerked around like you pulled him with a string. Maybe it was Jenny's eyes pulled him— she was looking at him. Not smiling, just looking. And she didn't look away. Didn't even blink till Farmer said something. Then she let her eyelids shut down slow, and Johnny swung back to the bar.

Amy laughed and flapped her left hand.

"Pretty ones always are," I said.

"Would you say she's pretty?" Amy asks, all the time wiping the counter in the vicinity of my arm while she's studying Jenny, taking her all in. Amy's taste ran more to false eyelashes than bare feet.

I gave Johnny an opportunity to get into the conversation, but he didn't take it.

"Yeah, I'd say she's pretty," I said after a bit, "but I run more to blue eyes and yellow curls myself."

Amy ran her dishcloth as close as she could to my hand without actually washing it and gave me the big smile.

I thought Johnny was miles away, but he heard and scowled sideways at us. Muttered something.

Amy and I made faces at each other to indicate we took his criticism under advisement, so I missed what was going on across the room till some of Jenny's lot started hooting and laughing and Johnny picks up his drink and saunters over.

Jenny was sitting with her eyes wide open. She didn't get the joke. Farmer was looking black. As I found out later, he did get it, and it was something Jenny said.

Johnny walks up to them.

Jenny smiles. She has this wonderful smile. That was the first time I saw it. I think it was Johnny's first time too.

"Egan's back," she told him with her eyes shining. "He was in school today."

The rest of them, but not Farmer, went off into howls of laughing again. Farmer looked blacker than ever.

"Egan!" a frizzy-headed girl hooted. "I sent him to the boss today for swinging at his brother with a window stick. And Jenny sits there telling us how beautiful the little felon is. My God! Egan, of all of them!"

"Egan's a friend of ours," Johnny says, real quiet, and I had to turn away so they wouldn't see me grin.

Then Farmer starts in sputtering, trying to fill the silence. "If you saw what we see... Walkabout little bastard! I'll walkabout him right into jail. Him and all the rest of them. I can do without ever seeing any of them!"

"They're coming in," Johnny says, like he enjoyed being able to spread good news. "We passed them breaking camp this afternoon."

There was a lot of groaning then, and Frizzy says they were hoping they'd got rid of that lot for good this time. As she says it, she's giving Johnny the benefit of about a hundred and fifty sparkling teeth.

He brushed her off like he brushed off flies, and turned back to Jenny.

Farmer, of course, didn't like it. "Better be getting home, Jen," he says, standing up real dignified.

She worked her feet back into her sandals and stood up too. She was almost as tall as Johnny. Very slim. Wearing a loose green dress that came almost to her ankles. Bare arms. Seemed to be all straight lines and big dark eyes.

"But Farmer!" Frizzy starts bleating. "You're not going home! You promised to stay and help us with the class lists!"

"Jenny can come home with us," Johnny says, and puts another cat among the pigeons. But he had Farmer where he wanted him that time.

Well, Jenny seemed perfectly content to be sitting between us in the old truck but she didn't say much, and when we got home she just thanked us and went into her house. Johnny went into our house and stood looking out a window.

I mooched around a bit, but he didn't move. Then I got cleaned up. When I was done that, he was still standing at the window.

I was getting hungry, so I took a box of crackers and a block of cheese out on the back verandah and sat on the top step. Two or three crackers later I brought out a couple of beers. Figured Johnny'd come out after he was done thinking, or whatever he was doing, and I might as well be prepared. But he didn't come.

The sun went down leaving the sky the colour of tangerines and the bush black against it.

Some little silver bats flitted from tree to tree.

After awhile a shadow materialized beside me. I pushed the crackers toward it and a hand shot out and took one.

Then nothing for awhile. Didn't seem to be anything at all going on but the two of us sitting there with our jaws working— till my next cracker flew out of my hand!

I jumped and swore. Thought it was a bat. But it was only a big moth. The kid breathed like he was laughing.

Then I saw him pick something from between his teeth and throw it away. Figured it wouldn't be food, so I laughed.

All the time the bats flapped lower.

Later, when a light came on over Jenny's door, the kid spoke. "That Mr. Greene, he big bloke."

"You scared?"

"Nah. I scared nothin'."

He picked up a stone that was lying on the verandah and shied it at the truck. It hit a hubcap with a sharp ping.

The sky faded and the full moon started rising.

The kid picked up another stone and tossed it up and down in his hand.

Well, there was this low shed behind our house with a narrow door at the far end. "Bet you can't hit that door," I said.

"Hit the knob."

"Aa-h!" I didn't believe it.

The stone left his hand and the doorknob fell off and rolled away.

"Not bad."

"Put the light out over Mr. Greene's door?"

"No, you'd scare Mrs. Greene."

"She scared."

He reached for my spare bottle.

"Young to be drinking beer, aren't you?"

"Nah."

I brushed away a moth. Then two or three. They were getting pretty thick.

Johnny came and stood just inside our screen door. I knew he was dressed for town. Wondered if I should tell him to come and have a beer with us. But before I made up my mind Jenny's door opened and she came out under the light.

"Oh-h," she said, very soft. Then her hands came up like a cup and she laughed.

She was wearing another of those long shapeless dresses of hers, only this one was white and seemed to have sleeves. She shook them and they quivered.

"Oh-h, Oh-h, Oh-h," she laughed.

Then she stretched out her arms. First one, then the other. Like dancers do. And she shook her head till her hair swirled around her.

I didn't hear our door open, but Johnny passed between me and the kid and went down the steps.

She ran toward him holding out her arms. "Look!" she cried. "Look!"

Her white dress had no more sleeves than the green one had and her hair was as heavy as ever, but there was a cloud of wings around her.

She twirled and Johnny caught her.

They laughed and danced together like a couple of little kids, and I never came so close to crying since I was ten and Ern...

A line of light cut across my hands, pale sunlight that must have been getting through a slit in Leona's awning.

"Where were you?" Ern was saying. "Look! There's a flower cart loaded with roses. Just look at all those wonderful colours. Let's go see..."

Jenny's roses were almost black...

I leaned against the pickup in the heat of afternoon and felt disaster coming.

Johnny came out of the Wooji Dairy, threw a few bags in the back, and climbed behind the wheel.

I didn't move.

"You coming?" he said.

"There's something going on," I told him. "I don't know what it is, but brace yourself because it's coming."

"I wouldn't be surprised," he muttered. "Come on."

I pushed myself away from the truck, and all the hairs on my legs stirred! It felt like something slid up my thigh and under my shorts, found the hollow of my back, and spread out into my armpits.

"Holy God!" I whispered.

I grabbed my bush hat off the back of my head and slapped at my legs and shoulders like I was fighting off an attack.

"Willy-willy," Johnny says. "Come on. We'll see where it is from up on the rise."

But it was more than willy-willy. Wind was roaring across the flats pushing a wall of dust ahead of it. Everything loose between us and the Far-Off Range was in it.

"Hold on!" Johnny yells.

He swung the truck back to the wind, and we got the windows up just before the storm climbed the rise and swept over us. Two seconds later we had a piece of tree up the back so big it took the both of us to lift it off.

Wooji was hit hard, and stars were hanging in the sky when we got home, to such a mess in our house we just went out and sat on the porch steps.

Thunder was banking in the west then. And there were shadows in the bush.

"Dogs," Johnny whispered.

"And kids."

A dog slunk down the yard.

Inside the other house, Farmer's dog growled.

At that, Farmer came to the door and looked out. "What's wrong, boy?" he said. "Something out there?"

The shadow-dog backed off, but three more were waiting among the trees.

Farmer opened the door and stuck his head out. Should've known better. His dog was down and bleeding into the dust before he had time to draw breath, and it was his own fault.

Then he saw us.

"You two bastards been there all the time!" he roared. "Watched the whole thing! Set the pack on him, didn't you! I'll see you pay for this!"

"Farmer, for God's sake," I said. "Don't be more of a fool than you already are."

He came charging across the yard and I went down to meet him, but he dropped before he took more than two or three strides.

The rock found him over the right eye just as thunder cracked all around us and the first rain fell...

Water dripped from the flower cart onto my foot.

"Look at the Gihon Beauties!" Ern was saying. "Aren't they lovely? Did you have flowers up to Wooji?"

"Sure," I said. "You should've seen the bush after that rain."

"What rain?"

"Wasn't I telling you about the rain?" I asked.

I tried to sound innocent. I wasn't about to admit my head was going in and out like a yo-yo.

"Thought I told you about that," I said. "Yeah, we had this storm, and two days later the whole place was blooming."

"I'd have loved that," she said. "What was it like?"

"Like?" I said. "Well... Like jumping in the canal with all your clothes on. Remember?"

She smiled.

"We even had two or three blades of grass in our yard," I told her. "Hardly knew the place. And Jenny's roses bloomed."

Ern buried her face in a big bunch of blossoms and breathed deep.

"What became of Jenny's roses?" she asked. "I mean, when you all... left..."

"Up there you have to be tough, Ern," I told her. "And they weren't."

She looked up and opened her mouth to say something then, but she howled instead. "This one's tough enough," she yelped. "Look what it did to my hand!"

There was a bead of blood on the ball of her thumb.

There was blood on Jenny's fingers...

We were laid off for a few days. Too hot to work. The company packed it in and we went home, just in time. Jenny was standing in the garden with tears streaming down her face, and it didn't take a genius to see the roses would never bloom again.

"They didn't belong here," Johnny says, and I never heard him talk so soft.

She looked at him with those big eyes, not trying to stop the tears or anything. "I know, but I loved them," she said.

It was enough to make even me cry.

Then she raised one hand to brush her hair back and you could see that the palm was bleeding.

Johnny's head snapped back when he saw that. He reached up and caught that hand, then the other one, and turned them over. They were both bleeding. Then, I don't know how it happened, but she was holding onto him and he was stroking her hair and calling her words I never heard before.

I turned away and left them...

By afternoon the Square was full of people that remembered me, and I got my hands shaken and my cheeks kissed till I lost count of the times. Told the same story and listened to the same story over and over again...

"Just down for a visit, Mrs. Albert..."

"Well, yes, Hank. Have to see Ern once in awhile, you know. Give her a chance to nag enough for another couple of years." (Big laughs.)

"Great to be back, Mr. Fagan. How's Ben?"

"Good, good."

"Been some changes," they told me. "Things keep coming round. 'Course most folks in the Square are new now. Just down from your neck of the woods." (Little laughs.)

"Yes, most of the old families are moving out. Moving up, they call it. Us oldtimers, though, we call it moving down. Down the Delta, you know, Arnold. Highrise, mostly. Wouldn't care for it myself..."

"Glad to see Erna stays. Place always looks nice, Arnold. Flowers helps..."

"You knew Mrs. Giberon died. Yes, laid her to rest last month..."

When we got tired and hungry, we ducked into a little eatery and I introduced Ern to fried minji, which is a kind of squash that grows in the hills. They cook it with bread crumbs and eggs, and it's not bad, when you get used to it.

Anyway the chairs in the cafe were comfortable.

Ern leaned back and stretched her legs. "It's been a nice day," she said. "Never knew I knew so many people. Thought most of them were gone... That's a cute little kid of Tracy Bloom's."

"Why don't you get married again?" I said.

"Me!" she hollered. "What about yourself!"

"Plenty of time for me," I said. "I'm only twenty-seven."

"Which makes me about a hundred and forty, I suppose!" she snapped.

"No," I said. "I know you're thirty-two. I guess I'd just like to know you were all right when I'm away."

"I can look after myself," she said. "What's got into you? I have my geraniums... And one of these days I'll have nieces and nephews."

"Maybe," I said.

She came back at me like a broken spring. "What's she like?"

I tried to make my face say, "What are you talking about, Erna?" but I could never put anything across my sister.

"Arnold!"

"Don't start me thinking about Missy," I said, "or I might catch the next barge up the water."

"Does she know?"

That's Ern, to ask a question you least expect.

"No."

"For heaven's sake, Arnold!"

"No," I said. "Her name is Missy. And that's all you're getting tonight."

"Aw, come on."

"Who's Baldy?"

She gave me a blank stare. Then she looked out into the Square. "Did you ever see so many mountain people?" she said. "They're everywhere these days. There's one now."

A straight-backed girl went by with the swing from the hips that gives them away every time. She had a small child in a sling over her shoulder...

Jenny was waiting against a backdrop of stars. The clan girl, our kid's sister, was huddled in the shadows of our verandah, holding her child in her arms.

"What's the matter?" Johnny asked softly.

"Baby sick."

"He's very sick," Jenny whispered.

"He die."

The child whimpered and the mother pressed her hand against his ear.

"Have you had him to the doctor?"

"Yes doctor."

"What did he say?"

"He say baby sick."

"Did he give you medicine for him?"

"Yes medicine."

Jenny pulled Johnny and me away a little. "He's so beautiful," she said. "You should see his little hands. And his eyes, so big and black."

"There's not much we can do, Jenny," Johnny said. "The medicine..."

"But he'll die."

"Poor little pup," I said. "Maybe he'll be better off."

"No!" Jenny cried. "No! Don't say that. She loves him. We can't just let him die. Please help. Farmer isn't here..."

We all knew what that meant! Farmer wouldn't help if he was right there in between us, and Jenny knew it.

"All right," Johnny said. "We can take him to the nuns. The doctor won't be in town for a couple of days, but the sisters know a lot about sickness. Maybe they'll be able to help him."

"Oh, Johnny," Jenny whispered. "Oh, Johnny, thank you. I knew we could count on you. I wish... Oh, I wish so many things. I wish I knew what to do... I... I wish I knew how to pray."

"I know," he said.

We all knew. She wished she could come with us, but she didn't dare. She wished she could help, but Farmer wouldn't let her. She wished she could heal the baby, but she didn't know how.

"Made you promise, did he?" I muttered.

"Never mind, love," Johnny said. "We'll take care of the baby."

"And if you like, afterward I'll come over and take care of your old man for you," I muttered.

"No, no, Arnold!" she cried. "No. You mustn't."

Johnny growled. "Don't you worry, Jenny," he said. "Arnold is not going to lay a finger on Farmer."

I knew what he meant, and it was going to happen one of these days...

"Where were you this time?" Ern wanted to know.

I shook my head. "Ern," I said, "you'd have a hard time believing. I was out under a blanket of stars you could reach down with your hands. I was revving up this battered old pickup truck. We were taking a little mountain girl and a dying child to a couple of nice old ladies with big, kind hearts. We were going to see if the ladies could stop the baby dying, knowing all the time they couldn't do it. Me. Arnold Grieve. From Red Dragon Square."

"I don't really know you any more, do I, Arnold," Ern said, very low.

"No," I said, "but don't feel bad about it, because I don't know myself. I mean, just now, remembering the sky the night the baby died, I suddenly saw the sky over the Square. I've been looking at it all my life, but..."

"I've never seen stars at all," Ern said.

"That's what I mean," I told her. "But for two days I been stretching out under the old flame tree and never noticed. Even looked right at it this morning watching Cranky circling, and still I never saw it. For two days I never noticed there's no shadows though it's broad daylight!"

Ern smiled. "Once, years ago," she said. "I must've been four or five. I made a picture of the Square in school. Naturally I gave it a yellow sky. And Miz Emerson... Remember her? Miz Emerson says, 'Come now, Ernie honey, you should colour the sky blue!' That was one of the shocks of my life! Miz Emerson not knowing the colour of the sky! Isn't it funny what you remember?"

She reached into her pocket for a tissue and blew her nose. Then she pulled her shoulders back. "I don't like you being a stranger, Arnold," she said.

"You better start talking. Tell me everything you know. About all the people you know. You. Missy. Johnny. Jenny. Wooji. All the places you ever been to. All the people you ever met."

I laughed. But she drew her chair in and leaned her elbows on the table and her chin on her hands. "I'm listening," she said. "Start anywhere."

At that moment the hill woman that made the fried minji came up and set a blue bowl of willow nuts between us. Willow nuts in their shells, dark and silky. They do that in the mountains after a meal. And out of the corner of my eye I saw the first one go by.

"Poor little bastard," I muttered.

"Who?"

I shook my head. "That Johnny, he good bloke," I said.

"No, Arnold!" Ern cried. "Come back! Don't go off again and leave me sitting in the Square looking at a bowl of chestnuts. Come back!"

"Willow nuts, Ern," I said. "Not chestnuts. And I'm all right. I just went back for a minute to the day the roof caved in."

I sighed. But my eyes rested on the blue bowl full of shiny, dark nuts, and looked right through it, all the way back to the desert road across the flats out of Wooji. Seeing it all again. Trying to make sense of it for Ern...

That day the kid came early. He arrived on our doorstep with the sun and actually knocked at the door. Usually he just came in whether we asked him or not. He was dressed neatly too— for him. And almost clean.

I went to the door and let him in. "What are you doing here?" I said. It was only two days after the baby died, and we knew his people usually went bush for weeks after a death, even of a small child.

But the kid hung his head.

"OK, if you don't want to tell me," I said. "Come on in."

"Come in and have some breakfast," Johnny called.

That did it! The kid went straight to the sink and washed his hands— without being told, which, if we didn't have a pretty good idea already, would've made it crystal clear that something unusual was up.

We were sitting at the table when he finished.

"Come and sit down," Johnny said.

Any other time the kid didn't need an invitation. That day he stood with his hands on the back of his chair and shuffled his feet.

We both looked at him, wondering what was going on.

"It's only bread and jam," I said. "Won't hurt you."

"Have to say first."

"OK. Say."

So he stood very straight, stared straight in front of him—and we didn't understand a word he said!!

"Try that again?" Johnny says.

We still didn't understand, but the second time we realized he wasn't speaking English.

"Thank you," Johnny says. "Now what does it mean?"

This time the kid hung his head like he did when he came to the door. "Mean, Johnny good bloke. Arnold good bloke," he muttered. "People say."

"Well, for God's sake!" I said. "Did you ever hear a better speech, Johnny?"

"No, I never did," Johnny says. "Thank you very much, mate. We're honoured."

The kid was already sitting down pushing in the bread and jam at that point, but he stood up when Johnny said that and took up the speech-making position again. "More," he says.

"More?"

"People say, Egan go school. Make promise."

Johnny laughed and gave the kid's head a shake. "A truly wise decision," he said. "We appreciate it."

We did, too. Knowing what it cost him, we wouldn't have blamed him for forgetting that second part altogether.

"Not scared," he told us.

"Of course not," I said.

And Johnny says, "Anyway, Farmer can't prove it was you threw that rock. Right after breakfast we'll go to town and buy you some new clothes."

Well, talk about lighting up! Christmas trees weren't in it with the kid's eyes when Johnny said that. "New?" he hollers. "Out of store?"

Poor little bastard!

And that was the start of a day none of us will ever forget. Every time I think of it, my blood boils.

It was a Saturday. A fine, warm, lazy Saturday in early winter.

When we got back from town I sat on the verandah with my feet on the railing reading the "Wooji Weekly Times." Johnny and the kid were down on the ground with a bucket of willow nuts, Johnny studying the kid's technique, trying to figure out how he could hit his mark every time.

Jenny was in her house across the yard. We could hear her singing as she moved from room to room. She probably wouldn't ever admit it, but we knew she never sang when Farmer was around. It was a sure sign— even better than his car being gone— and accounted for the kid being present.

I figured, on a nice Saturday afternoon Farmer would go to the pub and be gone till after sundown, which would be all right by me. But suddenly this motor starts roaring up the road and we all look up together.

"Sounds like Farmer's old bomb," I said.

Sure enough. Up the road he comes. Roars into the yard, jams on the brakes, and is in the house before we knew what hit us. "Jenny," he bellows. "Where the hell are you!?"

The kid melted around the corner of the verandah. I put my feet on the ground. Johnny's shoulders bunched and he flexed his hands.

"If there's one thing I will not stand," Farmer roars, "it's a dishonest woman! I told you to have nothing to do with that girl and her bastard brat!"

"She came to me for help!" Jenny cried.

"God save us!" he yelled. "She came to you for help! Are you the doctor? Are you the welfare? Whose idea was it to go to the nuns?"

"There wasn't anyone else," Jenny cried. "The doctor wasn't here. What else could we do?"

"You could bloody well do as you're told and mind your own business!"

"And let the baby die?"

"It died anyway, didn't it! And you would have spared me being the laughing stock of the whole of Wooji!"

"Who's laughing!" Johnny growled.

Farmer was near to choking he was so mad.

"I'm standing in the Dairy," he roars. "Just standing in the Dairy waiting to pay the milk bill. I'm feeling fine. Thinking I'm not doing too bad. Feeling good. When in comes that bloody little Sister Joyce, the one with the voice you can hear above Saturday night in the pub. 'Oh, Mr. Greene' she hoots. 'Good morning, Mr. Greene. How nice to see you, Mr. Greene. How's that dear little wife of yours, Mr. Greene? I was just saying to Sister Eveline what a sweet little wife you have. Taking an interest in the poor little baby. The one that died, you know. Trying to help the poor little fellow. Such a sweet girl!"

We couldn't hear much of Jenny's side of the argument, if she had one. But we could tell Farmer was tramping around in the house getting more and more beside himself.

"If he touches her, I'll kill him," Johnny said, very quiet.

"No, you won't, mate," I said. "It wouldn't look good at the trial. I'll do it. I'm not in love with his wife."

"Listen to me, Jenny!" Farmer roars. "You knew I didn't want you to have anything to do with that lot! And to make it worse, you went behind my back to Johnny Doyle!"

"I had to, Farmer!" Jenny cried. "I couldn't just let the baby die!"

"Well, he's dead now," Farmer snarls. "And good riddance. He'd grow up to be like that other one! The world would be better off without him too!"

"Stop it, Farmer!" Jenny cried. "Stop it! I won't listen to you!"

She ran out of the house and him after her.

He grabbed her arm.

She screamed.

He raised his other arm and hit her.

Johnny was across the yard and on the ground with her almost as soon as she fell, the same moment the first of the willow nuts struck.

The kid went for the eyes again, and it was hard for him to miss. That was what did it...

Sitting there over the willow nuts, Ern shuddered. "What happened to him?" she whispered.

"The cops caught up with him," I said. "Three days later."

"Yes. They'd have to."

"We did what we could. Got him a good lawyer. Testified at the hearing. He even wore his new school clothes! But the judge sided with the suffering husband. She slipped and fell, he said, and the attack was unprovoked."

"He was only a kid!" Ern cried.

"Yeah."

"They'll let him out, though."

I shook my head. "He was a free, wild boy, Ern," I said. "He couldn't live in prison."

Ern dug in her pocket for another tissue and we headed home as the early-evening lights were coming on.

"What I can't understand," Ern muttered, "is why she ever

married him in the first place."

"We make our own mistakes, Ern," I said.

She already knew that.

"I'll call Miz. Doyle in the morning," I told her.

"No!" she yelped.

"No!?"

"I mean, not tomorrow. She won't be home tomorrow. Don't call her tomorrow."

"All right," I said. "If you say so. But..."

"Give me one more day. Then you can call her. Please? Promise?"

I must've looked puzzled.

"Promise!"

"All right. I promise."

That satisfied her.

"I have to work in the morning," she said, "but I have a surprise for you in the evening."

"What is it?"

"It's a surprise!"

"Yes, but what? Are we going out? Staying home?"

"Out," she said. "Best clothes."

Chapter: 3

In the morning I turned out my pack. Knew I'd find a flat parcel tied with bits of yarn in the bottom. Hadn't looked at it since the grandmother put it in my hand as I was leaving the Meads, but I knew what it was. Smallest Granddaughter told me.

Smallest Granddaughter and I are best friends. We also have a business arrangement— I give her stale bread crusts and she gives me eggs from her geese. One bowlful of crumbs, one egg.

Generally she simply opens the window when she sees me coming and the exchange is made, but that morning she was waiting for me on the steps...

"I came to walk with you," she said, no other explanation being necessary between friends and business partners.

She tucked her hand in mine and skipped down the street-steps to the next level like she was about to spend the day. But when we turned the corner and the grandmother's house was out of sight, she stopped. "This is far enough," she said.

"House rules," I thought, and turned her around and started her back up the steps. But she danced out onto a retaining wall and came flying after me. "I know a secret," she whispered.

"Yes?"

"Yes. Grandmother is making you a present."

"Are you..?"

"No! I'm not supposed to tell you! But you might find out, and Grandmother would be sad. So you can't come into our house without knocking very loud upon the door."

I promised to knock very loud.

"It's a beautiful robe," she said. "The wool is white and soft, and we went far, far into the mountains to pick the flowers to make the blue for the trimming. Grandmother wants you to wear it when you go down the mountain. She says you will wear it with pride and... and... something I forget. Will you wear it?"

"I will wear it," I said, "with pride and whatever else Grandmother wants. And from now until I go, I will be careful to knock very loud upon your door."

"I don't want you to go!" she cried, and flung her arms around my neck...

I unfolded the robe and put it on. Never wore such a thing in my life before, but not bad. Not bad. Made me look taller, though I'm tall enough as it is. Seemed to blend with the tan of my skin and the sun-bleached streaks in my hair. Not bad at all!

Took it down the Square and had it pressed. This bored assistant took it from me and carried it into the back of the shop without a glance, but the tailor himself brought it back.

"Beautiful," he told me. "Beautiful. Handwoven, that. Master weaver's work and no mistake."

The grandmother would be pleased.

Then I took my sandals to be oiled. The shoeshine rubbed the leather with his thumb and told me, "Nothing like that nowadays. Never see it. No demand. Beautiful."

While I waited, I drank a cup of coffee in Leona's and watched the world go round and round the Square. Had the odd bad moment, wondering what Ern would say when she saw me looking like a mountain patriarch. Almost decided to see what Reg the Outfitter had for rent. But a guy in a pink-spotted tie came to the door of the shop and stood looking around. Put me off that idea. I'd take the word of the experts and wear the robe.

So when Ern came out to pick me up, I felt good. And when her eyes opened wide and she said, "Wow!" I figured I'd do, wherever we were going.

Ern had on this long blue skirt and a white blouse. No surprise there—she'd cut the skirt off at the bottom and wear it around the Square after. But I figured if Ern had gone even that far, I wouldn't be overdressed. Where was she taking me anyway!?

"Taxi should be waiting," she said.

I enjoyed the ride. Three years is a long time to be away from a city. New buildings up. Old buildings gone. Landmarks changed. Crowds of strangers in the streets.

I kept craning my neck to see everything, but Ern sat with her hands folded in her lap looking straight ahead.

"You look like the day we took the elevator," I told her.

"Don't remind me!" she snapped. "I don't know what I'm getting into. Never been downtown for... Oh, maybe four or five years."

"More like eight or ten," I thought. "Not since she had to go to the Town Hall for her divorce settlement."

So we were going downtown. Well, I already knew that. And when the cab stopped I knew we must be in Gihon Square, but I couldn't believe it. Last time I was there, Gihon Square was only a wet hole in the ground. Now... Boat harbour swaying with masts at anchor. Tidal lake with floating gardens and pavilions. Bridges. Belts of trees. In the distance a ring of white towers...

"In three years!" I said. "How far down did they go with the foundations?"

"Oh, for heaven's sake!" Ern laughed. "Who cares about foundations? Isn't it beautiful? I had no idea. Just look at that clump of irises against that japonica hedge. I should have come before!"

"Want to sit down and breathe it all in?" I suggested.

"No," she said, and took my arm. "No. We're going to the theatre."

"That can't be finished too!"

"The whole place is finished!"

I was impressed.

So we strolled around the north verge of the lake between the water and a marble wall that curved into the distance.

Here and there Ern paused to admire a flower, a clump of trees, a vine against the wall, but only for a moment, always moving on.

And that was how we came, almost without warning, to three pink quartzite arches, like stooping wings.

I stopped in my tracks.

"Nothing like that up to Wooji!" Ern cried.

Not Wooji. Penner's Rock...

The road followed the bed of a dry mountain stream. A few stunted pines clinging to piles of rubble. Granite boulders stranded on either side.

The storm that was coming was not far off. Even then, just after noon, the light was failing.

Nobody else on the bus but George. Johnny was sitting behind him, leaning forward to talk above the grinding of the gears. I was across the passage, trying to sleep. And the cat— he was down the back somewhere.

I was just dropping off when George turned and shouted, "Penner's Rock!"

I rubbed dirt and moisture off the window and looked out.

"No. This side," he said.

Over there, and just ahead, this large outcrop of rosy crystalline material was looming up. In the stormy light it looked like coals in a dying fire.

"Rose quartz," he shouted. "Biggest deposit in the world. Almost pure. Big order going down the Delta. Surprised we haven't met the trucks. But they know snow's coming."

We watched as the rosy glow came nearer. Besides that, nothing out the windows but deep pits in the gravel and piles of rubble as far as the eye could see through the murk.

"Hand work," George shouted. "Split out the stone with hand tools. Very dangerous."

We nodded.

"They say you can hear the screams of the dying!"

We laughed and George grinned.

"Never heard it myself," he said. "Only the wind... in the rocks."

He nursed the old bus up the valley and little by little Penner's Rock dropped behind.

When the road flattened out, he stopped and we looked back. Penner's Rock glowed, the only living thing in the valley.

I figured we were stopping to let the engine cool, and I said, "Aren't you going to turn her off?"

"What? Want to hear them, do you?"

"Why not?" I said. "How about a few minutes moving around? I feel like I been sitting here half my life."

"Sure," he says. "I might even join you... Always willing to take a chance."

Outside, the air was thin and clean, even with the storm upon us. We breathed deep and it felt good. I was beginning to feel at home in the mountains.

So I'm stamping around on the gravel. Taking the kinks out of my legs. Feeling born and bred to high country. Thinking Grieve, A., Red Dragon Square, Earth, Universe wouldn't be surprised by too much these molehills could dream up for his amusement, when this low moaning starts. Like the mountains are shifting at the roots and grinding on each other. And in no time at all the whole valley is shrieking.

We dove for the bus as the screams whistled over our heads and ricocheted off the peaks...

Damn! I'd been fine all day, but this new square was getting to me.

Ern was standing back smiling, though. Didn't seem to notice I'd been up to Penner's Rock for a few minutes, and I sneaked a sigh of relief.

"Beautiful," I said. "The stone looks liquid. And the lines don't end. Do you see how they rise?"

I almost took off again on those "infinite curves," but the thought of doing something to embarrass Ern, which she would soon let me know about, kept me on solid ground— if it was solid.

Arm in arm we passed under the middle arch onto a broad marble terrace. Before us, beyond a white balustrade, the full circle of the amphitheatre opened out.

"Breath-taking!" Ern whispered.

"Like an open-pit mine," I growled to myself. "Wonder how they keep her pumped out."

But Ern didn't hear me. Too busy moving along, taking everything in, calling my attention to this and that.

After a bit we passed a fountain where six or seven people were standing around talking.

"Beautiful," Ern said.

I turned to look again, and this man left the group and came toward us, holding out his hand. "Grieve? Arnold Grieve? Isn't it?" he said.

I recognized the voice and took the hand. "Hello, Councillor," I said... "My sister Erna."

He smiled at Ern and looked back like he was expecting a lady to join us, but she turned away.

"I came down alone," I said, knowing what he wanted to ask. "Some loose ends."

"And there's no chance?"

"No."

He shrugged. "Will we see you while you're here?"

"I haven't long," I said.

"Well, you know where to reach me."

We turned away.

"Did you see that gown!?" Ern whispered.

"Which gown?"

"Men! The one that girl was wearing. The one who turned her back. Ginger flower petals! That's what it's made of. Must have cost a fortune, and good for only once."

"That wouldn't bother Dee," I said.

"Johnny's sister!?"

"So-called. She's half-sister, step-sister— something. Su married her father when Johnny was eight and Dee must have been... oh, maybe twelve or thirteen."

Ern turned right around and looked again. But we were at a place in the balustrade where stairs went down to the seating levels and the landing was full of very young girls in white dresses trimmed with flowers. One of them danced up to us with a big smile. "I can show you to your places," she said.

We smiled back.

"I have to see your tickets first, though."

Tickets! I turned to Ern with a blank stare.

"I have them," she said, and held out two violet-coloured cards.

"Oo-o!" the child squealed. "You're my first guests to the Third Terrace. My sister will be green! She hasn't had any!"

She skipped ahead of us down the stairs, and heads turned.

"She'll be getting her head turned," I whispered to Ern.

"Think they're looking at her, do you," she says, out of the corner of her mouth.

"Sorry," I said. "You. Naturally."

"Don't be foolish," she snapped.

Down on the Third Terrace we had a table at the outer rim, right by the balustrade, also a waiter who brought us champagne and a tray of exotic bits of this and that to nibble. Treated us like visiting royalty. I wondered how Ern could afford it, but she was happy as a kid at a picnic.

A cally vine with purple flowers was taking hold of the balustrade right beside us. That pleased her too. "Our blues go perfectly," she said.

I looked at the vine and the uneasy feeling came again. Shook myself. Took a sip of champagne and leaned back. Let my eyes climb to the top terrace. Then let them swing down the circles of marble steps.

Shouldn't have done that!

Grabbed the balustrade and hung on. But the tiers above slowly revolved, and from below came a swirling sound, a water-swirling murmur.

I knew what was coming, but I couldn't stop it. The cally vine swelled till it hung overhead like a thick, dark forest, and I was sitting with Johnny and Dee on roots growing through a faded mosaic floor...

Dee dragged us along a broken path close to a wall that was falling bit by bit into an old canal. We were away down the outskirt islands where building first began.

Dee had been smoking those acrite cigarettes she used to like, and I was uneasy. I knew Johnny always gave her her own way when she was like that, but still I had this feeling we ought to get the hell out of there.

"Are you sure about this?" I argued.

"They're only harmless old bats in here," she said. "My father used to protect their interests, and I sort of inherited them. Not that I ever pay any attention to their mumbo-jumbo, so you needn't worry. Father believed in free thought, that's all, and didn't like persecution going on... Think I own the building, actually."

Johnny agreed with me. "I can think of a lot of things I'd rather be doing," he muttered, kind of testing the waters.

"You can do them after," Dee says. "This won't take long. They're always asking me to bring you. Want to see Su's cute little honey-boy now he's all grown up. So since you're here, you might as well get it over."

Johnny tried again. "Arnold has better things to do too," he suggested.

"Then Arnold can go and do them!" she snaps. "Nobody asked him. What is he, anyway? Your bodyguard or something? Make him go away. He can wait outside, for God's sake, if he must hang around."

She gave me this dirty look, but I didn't bite. Wasn't like I wasn't born on the canals, or never been down the City before. I mean, nobody in his right mind hangs around those old slums alone, especially with dark coming on, and I wasn't about to start the fashion!

I always gave Dee back as good as I got. "Slum landlord, are you?" I said. "Think you'd be ashamed to own up to it. This place ought to be condemned."

Johnny grinned. "It is condemned," he said. "How did you think she got so thick with the councillor?"

"It's not like that at all!" Dee says. "Jarl understands. I can't put the old things out while the seer's still with them. Father wouldn't hear of it. As long as the seer is with them, the place is theirs."

"But the seer is about three hundred and fifty already, isn't she?" I gave her back. "Seems to me like that's just a dodge..."

"Shut up!" she says, as she's pulling at a new-looking bell-rope that's hanging down beside a door that was new when her father's great-great-grandfather was a pup.

I expected squeaks and squawks from old hinges, but it was worse than that— the door opened without a sound, and this hand came out of shadows and grabbed my arm..

"Here you are at last!" this voice whispered. "We've been expecting you."

The hair on the back of my neck stirred. I mean, nobody told me we were coming!

"So glad," the voice kept on whispering. "So glad..." I think she called me 'child'— and I think it was a woman.

"So very gratified." I know she said that. Couldn't see why she'd be so very gratified to see me! Thought she must be taking me for Johnny till I heard something like, "the picture of his mother!"

After that she spoke a little louder.

"The seer has been wonderful all day," she told us. "Quite wonderful. Of course she knew! My dears, she may even speak! I really think she may. Now wouldn't that be lovely for you!"

Lord! Lovely!

Like the wall outside, the house was crumbling away. I heard slippage even as we were passing down this long corridor. Faint light came through slits, but they weren't windows. And air moved through arches that opened only to the wind. I slid my feet forward over uneven tiles, afraid of coming any minute to the step at the end of the world.

Away from the door the canal-water smell faded, and the heavy perfume of a cally vine in full flower surged toward us. They said the cally smell was poison. They said it would drug a man... hypnotize him... do terrible things to him.

Then we were in a courtyard and I was being pushed down onto the knees of the vine.

Stems disappeared upward into darkness. Branches as big as my arm spread outward. Roots buried themselves deep. And the scent was overpowering.

It was almost dark, but I heard clearly. A flock of cloister doves settled above my head. Shadowy men and women rustled, settling in the courtyard like the birds in the vine.

Someone put a drink in my hand, but I daren't touch it.

At last, when one by one my nerves were fraying, my head turned toward a faint whisper, and the seer was there, standing in the middle of the courtyard wrapped in a barge blanket, a green eyeshade on her head.

"Cold," she muttered. "Cold. Shadowed and cold. Shadowed... Cold a long time..."

The skin on my back crawled. It was a hot night, and humid, down there on swamp water.

I stirred and Dee gripped my hand. "Don't you dare move!" she whispered.

"Theatre... Amphi...theatre..." the seer muttered.

"The amphitheatre!" she shrieked, and the doves rose with a beating of wings like a drum accompaniment coming in a second or two too late.

I didn't move— couldn't— but Dee's nails dug into my palm.

"Grinding... on the plain. Stones of its cold... Cold stones gnawing... gnawing... And the people shuffling... round... round... shuffling..."

The voice strengthened.

"Over their heads! Over their heads, the arches. The gargoyles in the keystones... Look! They open their mouths... They cry..."

The voice faded again, running down.

"Cries... echoes... dry... old. Dry, old screaming... Dry, old screaming on the cold, old stones... And the ragged screaming..."

She was barely whispering, but my whole body screamed. "Come on. Let's get out of here!" I croaked.

"Wait!" Dee hissed.

A gasp.

The spell broke.

The seer crumpled onto the tiles.

The barge blanket folded like there was nothing in it. The green visor might have hidden empty space.

For a moment, nothing. Only Dee's nails digging.

Then the seer shuddered.

Her head came up.

"Wait!" she howled. "Wait! The message!"

Was she talking to me?

And a low laugh came out of her throat. It was like somebody else laughed.

"There is no message, fool!" a new voice cried, but from her mouth. "No message for those who shuffle. For those who go round... and round... and... round..."

That voice faded out too. But the seer raised her hands, her arms. The blanket fell back from her bones.

"Storm!" she cried then. "Wind! A path on the mountain! A young man, bent. Bent to the storm!"

Damn! I knew it. The message was for me. I knew it in my bones. The message was for me, and the message meant trouble.

The seer's arms arched above her head.

Her breath hissed in her mouth.

A long wail:

"No...

Wait...

Light...

We cannot follow into light..!"

She rose like she was pulled from above.

For a heartbeat she stayed like that, stretched, with her arms above her head. Then she was on the ground, still.

"Oh, my God!" Dee whispered.

She was pulling me to my feet, and I wasn't holding back...

When the vision faded an orchestra was playing on a little round stage below the level of our terrace, and Ern was investigating the tray.

I glanced around and the waiter came to my elbow. But all I wanted was for somebody to recognize him. Didn't they know who that was on the mountain?

Surely Ern would have known him. But a mime had replaced the jugglers and she didn't even look at me.

Slowly I began to breathe again. I was almost myself. And then the orchestra began a little tune that Johnny often sang, a song Su taught him.

The air around us softened. Water rippled into the orchestra pit till the musicians floated on a raft of lotus flowers. Translucent bridges, like arcs of light, flowed across the water. And on one of the bridges, a small figure in a white toga appeared. A small, slim figure with short, dark, curly hair.

A murmur swelled, died away.

Ern glanced at me and smiled. "Surprise!" she whispered.

Su took up that little tune that I remembered, and I don't think even my heart was beating at that moment!

Her voice might have been the voice of a child playing in sun and snow.

The child grew. Tested his strength on trees and rocks and water. He laughed and sang.

Hearing Johnny's mother sing those songs, I understood. That famous voice filled Gihon Square, but I only heard her heart. I knew the bond was strong between them, but I never knew how strong till then. It no longer seemed strange that she...

And then she began 'The Aspens of Eavenan.' Oh, God!

Ern looked at me with her eyes full of tears. "I had no idea," she whispered.

I bowed my head...

I was squatting on the ground. I was leaning back against the bole of a smooth old aspen, watching by the Mirror Pool under the autumn moon. All around the trees rustled, and yellow leaves floated down to settle on the water. Three fallow deer, like shadows, climbed the ravine. I heard the faintest click of hooves on stone...

"We're invited to the green room," Ern said. "Are you up to it? I don't know if I am or not."

"Dee knows we're here," I said, and she nodded.

We moved with the crowd. It seemed like half the City was trying to get into the green room. But even with the press of people around her, Su saw me the minute I passed through the door. Her eyes opened wide, and her glance swept past my shoulder.

I shook my head. Then I walked up to her and wrapped my arms around her. "He's fine," I whispered. "Working hard and singing loud. But not here."

She gave me a big hug, and I don't think a soul in the place guessed what she was feeling.

"You'll come and see me tomorrow," she ordered. "I'll send the car. Early!"

"Yes, Ma'am," I promised. "Whatever you say, Ma'am."

"Don't be impertinent!"

She was laughing, but I held her long enough for her to blink away the tears that filled her eyes.

As I left her and saw the people that had fallen back to let me through, I was surprised. I mean, I knew who they were, and what surprised me was that none of them wanted to know who the hell I thought I was. I enjoyed that! Must have been the grandmother's robe!

Ern and I didn't talk much on the drive home. Once Ern said, "Johnny's sister spoke to me. She doesn't like you."

"Never did," I said. "Blames me for taking Johnny away."

"So she said. 'In that case,' I said to her, 'we have a lot in common, each of us with a bad influence for a brother!"

We got out of the taxi at the top of the Square and walked home, to put Gihon Square behind us.

In the alley, a young bargee lurched past us.

"Awful lot of acrite around now," Ern said. "Never used to be so much. Spoils the place."

"Stay away from that stuff!" I warned her.

Chapter: 4

Nothing spoiled Su's place.

Up The Dykes you never bumped into bargees full of acrite lurching by. You never heard crankybirds squawking either— Su's trees were full of merrybells flitting around. Her air smelled of jasmine, not barge canals. And when you sat in her deck chairs, you didn't look at old brick warehouses, or split the fabric every time you moved.

The next morning we sat on the south patio in the shade of an umbrella tree looking over half an acre of clipped grass, and I thought of my house up the Meads, where I wash in the kitchen and eat in the bedroom— or sleep in the dining room, whichever. And supply myself with eggs by reaching through the front door into the Grandmother's window! Not that I'll always live like that....

"Pull yourself together, Arnold," I thought. "This grilling isn't going to be easy. Keep your wits about you."

"You look well," she said first. "Older. You have a new... authority about you. I suppose Johnny too..."

It was on the tip of my tongue to say, "If you think I have authority, Miz Doyle!" But I changed it to, "It's been almost three years."

"Is that all," she said, with this funny smile.

Then she took a deep breath. "I'm grateful for this visit, Arnold," she told me. "I want to thank you for all you've done. And Erna too. Erna has helped me very much and I've never thanked her properly."

"I don't think she'd agree," I said. "Last night was a rare treat."

"Was it?"

"Oh, yes."

"And you still have your crankybird?"

She was having a hard time getting started. A surprise to me! Maybe it was my new authority.

"What do you know about crankybirds?" I said, to lighten the mood. "Your shell-like ears are far too pink for the squawks of crankybirds!"

She laughed. "I have done very well, Arnold," she said. "But I've been in places like... places like Red Dragon Square before. And I remember a crankybird or two."

"My cranky's a fine specimen," I said, and gave her a big smile, but she didn't notice.

Instead she sat very straight with her hands in her lap, watching a pair of merrybells across the lawn.

"Arnold," she said. "Arnold, you know I never pry..."

Now we were getting down to it. "Careful," I warned myself. But she threw me anyway. "Have you been to the hospital?" she said.

Then she looked at me sharply, not to miss the effect.

"Not yet," I said, to give myself time. She wasn't supposed to know about the hospital. On the other hand, I wasn't supposed to lie to her either.

"Why didn't he tell me!" she cried. "Surely he could have told me. I would have understood. I could have shared it with him. I knew he was going to the City every morning that last time when you came home from... from up-country, but..."

She waved one hand like she was trying to clear something away. Something she didn't like. Up-country, I guess. It was all the same to her.

"Miz Doyle," I said. "It's all right. How did you find out about Jenny?"

"I have my ways," she said. "Then about a year ago an accountant I didn't know called, asking if he should continue making the payments from Johnny's bank."

"He didn't want to leave her in a public ward," I said.

"She's very beautiful."

"Yes."

It was a weak moment. Su could have had anything she liked out of me then, but she was feeling too sorry for herself.

"He should never have gone near those hills!" she cried. "They do things to people. Hurting things. I knew how it would be!"

"He loved the hills," I said.

I guess something in my voice stopped her.

"Well, then," she said, "all right. We won't worry about that now. There's so much I want you to tell me."

Then she looked right at me. "Truthfully, Arnold," she said.

I nodded. "I promised him I would," I told her.

"He was so changed when he came back from... Wooji," she said. The word was out.

"Losing Jenny was very bad," I said. "It still is."

She looked up quickly and opened her mouth like she was going to say something but thought better of it. Instead she looked across the lawn again.

"He remembered a place in the mountains," she said, "where the trees grew very straight and tall and the sun in the evening cast long, thin shadows on the ground."

"We been in lots of places like that," I told her.

"No, no. This was a special place. He was there with me. Many years ago. He was only five when I brought him from the mountains, you know. But he remembered that place."

"Oh," I said. "The place he first... I mean, that was where he met the old man and... the cat... I guess."

Lord love us, that was close! I almost used the animal's name!

She didn't seem to notice. "He was so little and foolish," she cried, "and that old man was going to let him touch... He was putting his fingers into that great beast's mouth when I rescued him."

"You and I have rescued him many times, Miz Doyle," I said, "but then I think you should have let him go. He was in no danger there."

"You too!" she cried. "That monster towered over him. He was only a baby!"

"It liked him."

"Arnold, please. You're believing his version."

"The sun was almost down," I said, "and the shadows were sharp against the ground. Everything was gold-coloured. And the cat's eyes were golden. He had never seen yellow eyes before."

"That old man should have known better than to take his cat into a place where there might be people," she wailed. "That was a terrible thing to do."

"Johnny says they came to see him," I said.

"They didn't know a thing about him!" she cried. "They were just there. Hoping for a handout, I suppose."

"He says they loved him very much, and the cat blinked at him and purred."

She looked at me blankly. "That's what he said the day he first talked of going back," she whispered. "We'd been over that story a thousand times before. But that time... He said, 'I think I'm going back, Su.'"

"He never had a choice," I told her.

"Nobody goes back to the mountains!" she cried. "It's the other way around. You know it is, Arnold. The mountain people stream into the City every day."

"And go round and round," I said. "Round and round and round..."

Her eyes widened.

"It wasn't easy for him either," I said. "We got into an awful lot of trouble trying not to have to go."

She looked up as if she really wanted to believe that, so I stuck my neck out a little for her.

"Remember that black jacket with the gold buttons he had? He gave that to a bum in a tavern down Chitown. Forced it on him. God only knows why! That was the night Dee lost a fancy pair of shoes too, that she never forgave me for.

They wanted to go to the beach so I took them to a place I knew on the Main Stream where there was sand."

I laughed. "That was the night we all ate scampi and freet and Dee was sick. Which she never forgave me for either!"

"Dee's married now," Su said, but she sounded like she wasn't much interested.

"Johnny will be glad," I told her. Dee used to get into more trouble than either of us. But anything to do with Johnny...

"Came from the mountains, Su and I," Johnny said. "Everybody came from the mountains one time or other. Nobody ever goes back, though. Did you know that, Dee? Did you know that, Arnold? Nobody ever goes back."

"That's right," Dee said. "Nobody. Ever. You remember that."

"Have to," he said. "Have to go back to the mountains."

"Nah!" I said. "You and me'll go back up to Wooji after blue-rock and make a mint of money."

"No. No. Have to go to the mountains. Find the winter. Keep the yellow snow, I think it is. Promised I would..."

The jasmine leaves stirred.

"Dee took it very hard," Su said. "She's terrified of the mountains. She didn't want Johnny to go any more than I did."

"Johnny wasn't like that, Miz. Doyle," I said. "You should've seen him up to Wooji. Nothing stopped him. Not heat, nor dust. Storms. Work. Nothing. He took it all and laughed— at first. He was different in the City."

"Of course he was different in the City!" she cried. "He was clean and civilized, and properly fed and cared for."

"No," I said, "I didn't mean that. We had showers up to Wooji, and good friends, and we ate good food. I mean Johnny laughed a lot, and thought up things to do, and made jokes. At first."

Su shuddered. "Heat shimmer off tin rooves, and salt sparkle on the ground," she said.

"Johnny loved it."

She sat a long time without speaking after that, and I watched the merrybells to give her time to get rid of the tears that kept coming to her eyes.

"I drove myself mercilessly for Johnny," she said after awhile. "He was only a baby when I brought him here. I didn't want him to grow up in the cold, and wind, and struggle of the mountains. I wanted him to have a good, warm, comfortable life down here."

It was my turn to be quiet.

"Well, answer me," she said. "You know I was right."

"No," I said. "No. For a while it was my job to look after him too, so I know. He could never be like that. He..."

"You're talking to his mother!" she cried.

I shook my head. She didn't want to understand. And if she didn't want to, I didn't know how to make her.

"He sat on the patio day after day," she said. "Facing the sun and the mountains. Not seeing anything. Not seeing anything at all. Just sitting."

I knew. I'd been through it with him.

"Sometimes in the evenings he would talk to me about Jacon Jaconi— he's a mythical figure in Jaconi legend."

"I've heard of him," I said with a smile. "He's the guy had the guts to turn right around and go back. Just made up his mind to go, and went. Bag and baggage. Wives, kids, and pack mules. Johnny kept telling me too."

"I argued with him," Su said. "I told him nobody goes back today. I told him there isn't even a road now. But he didn't believe me."

"I know," I said. "There had to be a road."

"He began to rummage in libraries. He read old manuscripts. He poured over moldering maps."

"I know. He was looking for the point where myth becomes reality. There had to be truth in the old legends. Once you got to the end of the marshes... Once you got back to the hills... Up where the river ran clear you would find Derr and Eulu still standing over the Moonstream."

"The Moonstream!" she cried. "It's a song! A story!"

"No," I said. "No. I used to think so too. But we slept on Derr one night and watched the moon rise over Eulu and shine down on the river."

She gasped.

"Yes," I said. "Two mountains side by side. And the river in the middle. The local people call it the Hellish."

"Then of course it isn't the Moonstream!" she cried. "It's just..."

I shook my head. "You know the songs, Miz Doyle," I said.

"Yes, I know the songs," she said. "That's what they are, songs. And my son left me..."

"It wasn't easy," I said.

"I should hope not!"

"No, I mean even if he wanted to. The first time, he went around in a circle. All he found out was that the bridge was out at Hawberry. Ended up in Red Dragon Square."

"He should have come home to me!" she cried.

"No," I said. "No. He couldn't. I was looking after him then..."

It was afternoon, and hot in Red Dragon Square.

Johnny and I had put in a long night, after that first time he tried to get away, and he was still dead to the world in the sleep-out. I was on the sofa trying not to wake up.

I laid there dozing and dreaming. Finally opened one eye, and this little lizard was peering at me from the windowsill. Blinked, and it slid a foot or so along the wall.

A jug of jilly was standing on the table. Ern must've left it. Had a deep puddle around it and dripped when I picked it up, but I poured some into a glass and drank it.

Poured some for Johnny too. And I'm half way through the screen door, everything going fine, when this scrubby little monk starts up the alley. Looked a lot like the lizard, that monk— dingy-white cassock, eyes darting side to side. Not making a sound either. Wouldn't be. Hour of Silence, midafternoon.

Sees me coming through the door, and out come the hands out of the big loose sleeves. He's making this little blessing motion in the air. Just being neighbourly. Knows me.

Doesn't know Johnny, of course. Doesn't know anybody else is there. I don't know myself, till Johnny takes a few lurching steps out into the yard. He is not a pretty sight!

The monk breaks his stride and his jaw drops.

"What's the matter?" Johnny says, real nasty. "You see before you the sacrificial lamb, that's all. Did you never see a sacrifice before?"

The monk is still staring, and he starts in with the blessings and doesn't stop, like his brain forgot to turn his hands off.

"The Lord moves in mysterious ways," Johnny mutters. "Picking on women and children."

At that the monk turns the colour of his dress and flops down on his knees right there in the alley. He's praying like his life depended on it. I didn't think Johnny looked that bad!

I guess Johnny didn't either.

"Get up," he says. "Get up and look me in the face."

"Mercy, mercy," the poor little goon squawks.

He would've done better clearing out, but he had to open his mouth, silence or no silence.

"We do not mean to offend," he says. "We are but humble servants... Our work is to comfort His suffering children..."

"What's the matter then?" Johnny hollers. "Don't know where they are? Stick around with me, I'll show you! I know where they are!"

"His will be done," the monk whimpers. "Kneel with me..."

"Kneel?" Johnny snarls. "Kneel? Me? What about the roses, humble servant? Tell me about the roses. Where was your God when the roses needed him? And the baby? And our kid, poor little bastard. Where was your God when they put our kid in prison? Where was he when Jenny broke her heart?"

Then he filled his lungs with hot alley air, and the voice that came out of him could have been the voice of the Red Dragon himself.

"I am Jaconi of the mountains," he roared, "and I say your God is a fraud and a liar. He can rot in Hell before I'll kneel to him."

His voice dropped. "Get out!" he growled. "Out... Before I kill you."

I can still hear the bang of the screen door as I shot out onto the verandah. But it was all right. The monk was galloping down the alley the way he came, holding his skirt above his knees and hollering like all the dragons that had the afternoon off were chasing after him.

"Come on," I said. "We'll go back to Wooji."

"No, I don't think so."

"Suit yourself..."

I must have spoken out loud.

"Forgive me, Arnold," Su said, like she'd been away off somewhere too. "Johnny has gone from me, and I have a very deep sadness in my soul. I've tried to understand, but..."

"Miz Doyle..," I said.

Then I stopped with my heart hammering. I knew what I was about to say, and I couldn't believe it.

"Miz Doyle," I said again, "I'll be here a few more days. Then I'm going back. If you want to come with me, just you say the word."

She looked at me, but I couldn't read her face. Then she got up and left.

I lay back in my chair in a cold sweat and shut my eyes. It must have been that feeling that reminded me of the last day at Dee's place...

"We'll take the St. Simeon Bridge," Johnny said. "The one over the north weir is out."

So we took the long way around by the Fens Road. Shimmering saltmarsh and vapour. Never my favourite place, the Depthmire, and walking across the footbridge to her gate with the water in the channel sucking and gurgling, I wanted to turn around and run. I mean, I was born on the Delta, but not down there where you feel like you're walking on jelly.

"We're out by the pool," Dee called. "Come and have a drink."

Her place looked nice, but the floor of white beach pebbles was new again and for a minute I was almost sick. Hardly dared step on them. Felt like I was teetering on a pile of white stones rising out of ooze from bedrock, and any minute they were going to slide out from under me.

Jarl was there, floating in the water. "Thought you weren't coming," he said.

"The bridge was out over the north weir," Johnny told him.

"The whole place is out," he growled, as he pulled himself out of the pool. "I keep telling Dee. Any day now this place is going to sink right out of sight. But she'll just add a few clam shells to the decor and go right on coming here."

"I like it," she snapped.

"Never should have allowed building on these fens," Jarl kept on. "Dredging new channels in this muck. It's insane. And more of these expensive hideouts all the time. One high tide with a good stiff wind behind it..."

"The weirs take care of the tides," Dee argued.

"The weirs are supposed to take care of the tides, but they never do. The water comes too high, and the mud is subsiding. You know the pilings for the boat dock are constantly having to be replaced. And now Johnny says the north weir bridge is out."

"Oh, shut up, Councillor," Dee snapped. "Have a drink. You're morbid."

Out beyond the Depthmire a large white vessel moved slowly toward the Main Stream docks. A boat purred by in the channel.

I lay in a sun-chair trying to relax, but tensed up, wanting to get away. If I let my mind wander, though, the place was a little easier to take, so I thought about what it must be like being rich and the time passed.

But as the sun sank into the fens and the thermal screens began to sigh, the sucking and gurgling in the channels deepened.

"Tide's turned," Jarl said, and rose to his feet. "Come and look at the boat slip."

I roused myself and strolled after the Councillor and Johnny around the pool, through a gate in the wall, and out to the slip where Dee's cruiser was moored. The running tide was swirling around the piles and the boat rocked and creaked.

"Every tide undermines the mud a little more," Jarl said, and kicked at the moorings. "I loathe this place. It isn't safe. Try and get Dee to give it up, will you, Johnny? She'll listen to you. God knows she won't take my advice."

I turned away from the water. Now that the tide was dropping, the mud banks were beginning to stink, and I wanted to run even more.

We all turned back. Then there was this frightened little cry, and this fruit basket, barely still afloat, swept around a bend in the channel on its way toward the sea. Clinging to its rim was this muddy, half-drowned kitten.

Johnny kicked off his shoes.

"My God, Johnny!" Jarl shouted. "Don't go in there."

I couldn't believe he was doing it. All the horrors I ever heard of leapt into my mind. Mud sharks. Conger eels. Leaches big as a man's hand...

Eventually we pulled him out and Jarl hosed him down with warm water. But he wouldn't give up the kitten.

After we cleaned him up, Dee rubbed antiseptic on the scratches and screeched at him to wake up, to wake up for God's sake!

"Jenny?" he said.

"Oh, my sweet love!" she whimpered. But she slapped him, good and hard, all the same.

He opened his eyes and smiled. "What's the matter?" he says.

"You were so far away!" Dee hollers. "Don't you ever do that to me again!"

He rubbed the kitten against his cheek. Then he put it in her hands. It was a cute little thing with ginger fur fluffing up nice as it dried.

"Good-bye, Dee," he said, and kissed her...

I left The Dykes early in the evening.

Su stood with me for a few minutes looking out over the City under its pall of vapour. Here and there the setting sun reflected back fire-red, and away to the south sluggish delta water gleamed coppery.

"I've always liked this view," Su said, but as if she was beginning to wonder why.

I didn't say anything. Instead I turned toward the hills. Up there the light would be silvery. Smallest Granddaughter would see the stars as she said her prayers at the loft window. I hoped she wouldn't forget to mention me.

"I won't be staying long," I said. "I'm getting homesick."

Chapter: 5

Next morning I stood a minute outside the bronze gates that led into the hospital garden, bracing myself for the ordeal ahead. This would be the worst.

As I stood there, a guard in uniform lounged up to me.

"Morning," he said. "Nice-day-fer-the-time-a-year. Were you wanting to visit somebody?"

"Jenny Greene," I said. "Mrs. Jenny Greene."

He looked at me with interest. "Don't get more than one or two for Mrs. Greene," he said.

"Husband never comes?"

"No. Never seen no husband. Probably took his divorce and cleared off. Most of them do."

"Sounds like Farmer," I muttered.

"Farmer?" he says, grinning. "Farmer Greene? You're kidding!"

"No... There'll be a lady joining me."

"Sure. Just wait in the garden where I can see you. Meanwhile I'll let them know you're coming. Have the little lady ready for you."

I walked along a path between tall cypress trees till I came to a red bench and sat down.

I sat facing the gate, watching for Su, so at first I didn't see anyone on the other side of the trees. Heard her singing though, when I stopped moving around. And located her in a bed of pansies watching me as she sang. She sounded like a little girl, though she must have been ancient.

Her song was sad, but her eyes were bright enough.

"Poetry, you know," she chirped, when the song ended.

"Poetry?"

"That I was singing now," she said. "Lost love. And winding sheets. And death. The cypress trees remind me. But I don't know... They use winding sheets in here, you know. When people die."

"No," I said. "I didn't know."

"Oh, yes," she said. "Do you like my ring?"

She held up her hand for the light to catch the stone, but there was no stone. No ring.

I shivered.

"I hope you like opals," she said, still looking at the ring. "Some don't. Some think they're evil things, but I have never found mine so. Of course, today I'm only Marion 13. Perhaps tomorrow, when I'm 59 or 60— you see I count very well... How-do-you-do?"

I got hold of myself. "Hi," I said, and smiled.

Her eyes twinkled. Her face reminded me of a dried apple, and her hair fluffed out around it like it would blow off if there was a little puff of wind.

She stepped out of the pansies and came closer. Seemed to take to me.

"I knew the moment I saw you, you were a one to walk right into a bloodstone and take it by the heart," she said. "My John was like that. He had no fear of them, not one drop. Of course he didn't! Wouldn't give me bloodstones if he did, would he!"

She giggled and perched on the bench beside me. "You didn't come yesterday," she said.

"No," I agreed. "I didn't make it yesterday. I had things to do."

"What's more important than coming here!?"

"To tell the truth," I said, "I was visiting a lady. Are you angry with me?"

"Johnny was dead, you see," she told me. "Dead, under the tractor."

"I didn't know," I said.

"Oh, you did know," she scolded. "Of course you did."

"Oh, yes," I lied. "I think I remember now."

"Of course you do."

I couldn't think of anything to say, but evidently I wasn't expected to.

"I shall be going home soon," she told me. "Home under the mountains. Where the chickens are. And John... under the tractor."

Then Su appeared.

Marion gasped when she saw her. "Johnny!" she whispered.

Su was dressed in faded jeans and a white shirt, and at that distance passed for a boy.

"Did it hurt you very much?" Marion called out to her.

She jumped up and ran toward the gate.

My heart froze, but Su didn't even flinch as the hand that wore the ring touched her face and hair.

"Your hair is still the same," Marion said. "Still black and beautiful and full of springy little curls."

Su took the hand that caressed her head and held it as we all moved slowly along the path.

"My hair is a sorry mess, I fear," Marion giggled, "but I shall brush it when we're home and wash it in water from the mountains, and it will shine again."

She looked eastward. "Sometimes I can see the mountains," she said. "From my window. When the shadows come. And once, on a winter evening, there was snow."

"I wish I could see that," I muttered.

"Oh, then you must go where the snow is!" she cried, and she grabbed my arm and pinched. "You must go there. Then you can guard the shadows. And keep the yellow snow!"

So that was where Johnny got the yellow snow from. Old Marion sent him too.

"That sounds like a good idea," I said. "I'll help the one that went before. Remember him?"

She thought a moment. Then she looked at Su. "That was you!" she cried. "Did you find it?"

Su's mouth opened, but before she could get a word out, I said, "Sure he did. He found it, and he's keeping it right now. He made arrangements. Everything is in good hands."

Marion danced a little step. Then she skipped along the path ahead of us and disappeared. I thought we'd seen the last of her, but just as we reached the lawn at the end of the path she popped out of a bush and whispered, "Remember! Left to right! Always left to right!"

Round and round.

And always left to right.

My God!

We found Jenny sitting in a window in a blue gown, her hands in her lap. It was a large, high window with no curtains, and the light was strong behind her.

I stopped still in the doorway I was so surprised to see her there. I guess I expected her to be in bed or something. I don't know what I expected. Certainly not this. She seemed almost like her old self, except quieter, stiller.

She looked up when she heard us and her eyes widened. For a minute I think she thought Su was Johnny. Then she saw me and blinked.

"Hello, Jenny," I said.

"Arnold!" she murmured, but her eyes slid by me like Su's did after the concert.

I walked up to her and took her hand. "Johnny's fine," I said. "Better looking than ever. Still waiting for you."

She smiled then, the old heart-wrenching smile that always got to anybody that loved her.

"I don't know where he is," she said. "Do you know where he is, Arnold?"

Her speech was a little slow and she seemed to think slowly.

"I know where he is, love," I said.

"May I go there?"

She asked like a small child, and I think she would have accepted a "no" answer without question. But the smile she gave me when I heard myself tell her "yes" more than made up for the "Lord-help-us!" feeling that knotted up my stomach.

For a few minutes we sat side by side in the window and she was quiet, withdrawn.

"This is not right!" I thought. "Jenny did nothing wrong. There is no cause for her to suffer. Her beauty and... and... I don't know... Whatever it is that makes her Jenny... Those things can't be touched by the Farmer Greenes of this world. Jenny is beyond that."

As I looked at her and held her hand, I understood a little what Jenny was, what Johnny loved, what it was we needed up the Meads.

Suddenly she looked up and began to speak.

"Three shadows came to drink at the pool," she said. "Then they whisked up the ravine. I think they were deer."

My skin prickled. I remembered!

"We watched them go," she said. "Then I knelt by the pool and looked at my face in the mirror."

She raised her hands and held back her hair like she was holding it out of water.

"Who is Jenny?' I asked him.

"Jenny is my love," he said.

"She must be very old," I thought. "I don't know the face in the mirror."

"It's only the ripples," he said.

"But there are no ripples in the Mirror Pool."

Then she took hold of my hands in a strong grip. Her voice was stronger too.

"Was there a time before, Arnold?" she said.

I hesitated.

"Was there? Under the trees? Where little silver flying things were? And moths with wings on fire?"

"Yes."

"Yes... But it went away."

She clutched my hands.

"It was all very long ago, Jenny," I said.

"And now I am old."

"Not as old as all that," I said, and smiled. "It only seems... because..."

"And he... he..."

"He loved you, Jenny," I said.

She trembled.

"There was a tiny boy," she whispered. "My baby. And he died."

"No, Jenny," I told her. "No. You're forgetting."

Her eyes held mine. No tears. Just questions.

"He was the child of a girl we knew," I told her. "You loved him very much."

"But he died."

"Yes."

She was still as the stream in the heart of the Mirror Pool, but I could barely control my emotions. She was understanding. Her speech was coming clearer, quicker.

"Why, Arnold?"

I didn't know what to tell her. I never did know. All I could think of was the way the mother howled that night. I'd learned a lot in three years, but I still didn't know...

"Why did my baby die?"

"Not yours, Jenny."

"Yes, mine. Yes. Part of me. I loved him. I wanted him to live. I prayed in the dark when... when... I said, 'God, don't take the baby away.'"

"I know, love."

"Remember his little hands, Arnold? The little fingers? And the tiny fingernails?"

Her body went tense.

"Johnny!" she shrieked. "Shut your eyes! Don't look! Don't let it come!"

"No! Jenny!"

She shook with sobs.

"There was dirt under his fingernails," she cried. "And his ears ran puss. And his nose. Thick and green. Dead! Dead, Johnny!"

I held her close. If she thought I was Johnny, I would be Johnny. And my mind and my soul fought back, as his would fight. "No. This is not true. This cannot be. This is a mistake and it must end. It must end now!"

I had learned that much.

"I'm so afraid, Johnny," she whispered. "I go round and round in my mind, and everything changes."

"Not everything, Jenny. Not the stars. Or the silver bats. Or... me."

"Things come to me," she said. "Beautiful things. And then they change and they're dead... With blood on them, and holes in them..."

"Hush, Jenny."

"Why, Johnny? Why? When I love them, why do they change so I can't look at them?"

Her voice shrilled and I held her tight.

"Johnny loves you, Jenny," I said. "That doesn't change."

"But when I need him, he doesn't come. And I'm afraid he's dead too. Is he dead, Arnold?"

"No. No, love. Alive. With him everything is alive now. The other was a long time ago."

"On the other side of the moon."

"And now we have a good place."

"Would my roses grow there?"

"I'm sure they would."

"Perhaps the baby smells them and picks them. No, Johnny! He mustn't pick them and scratch his fingers!"

"He won't scratch his fingers, love."

"There would be holes, with blood in them! And he would change!"

"Jenny. Listen to me. Listen to me, Jenny. There is a path on the mountain. We found it. It's a good path that leads to a beautiful valley. I'm going to take you there."

"Is Johnny there?"

"Johnny is there," I said. "Waiting for us."

"No more hospital?"

"You won't need the hospital any more," I told her, and I knew I was right.

She looked over my shoulder at someone. Not Su. Another person. And I turned my head and saw her doctor watching us. She smiled. "I'm better, Doctor," she said. "I'm going... home."

The professional mask broke up, became astonishment.

He looked at me. "But you're not..." he started.

Then Su spoke for the first time. "Perhaps you will have someone pack Mrs. Greene's things, Doctor," she said. "It is my son's wish that Jenny join him now. She will come to me today."

She took him by the arm and led him away.

"That is Johnny's mother," Jenny said.

"Yes."

"She came to see me sometimes. I remember..."

I laughed. That was Johnny's mother, all right. Johnny's mother in action, cutting through problems like they didn't exist. You can do that when you're a Su Doyle. And Jenny was out of that hospital and up The Dykes as easy as if we'd practised it for months.

Before I knew where I was, I had my instructions for the next few days and I was sitting beside Harry, Su's houseman, being driven home.

When I stopped clutching my head, about half way to the Square, I started to laugh. And by the time we got there, both of us were in pain. Harry was all wet down the front from the tears he didn't dare wipe away for fear of blurring his vision. And I was so sore across the stomach I thought I'd never stand up straight again.

Neither of us knew what the joke was. Not even me! So I suggested we stop in the Square for a cold drink and sober up, which we did.

Harry spent the time telling me how wonderful Miz Doyle was. Couldn't say enough in praise of her. I wasn't quite so sure, but I figured I was stuck with her and might as well get used to it.

After Harry left I started up the Square. It was getting dark and I figured Ern would have eaten already without me, but I met her coming down the alley and we went to Archie's for a meal. I hadn't had much to eat all day, and I was hungry.

"So how did you make out at the hospital?" Ern started in when we finished the soup and I began to feel better.

"Fine," I said. "I'll be taking her back with me."

"Who? Su?"

"Jenny."

Ern looked at me like I'd gone stark staring. "You can't do that!" she hollered. "How are you going to look after her?"

"What do you mean?" I said. "Jenny won't be any trouble."

By then Ern was sure I was crazy. "Arnold, sweetheart," she said, "are we talking about the same girl? Jenny Greene?"

"Yes," I said.

"But she... She has to be fed. And dressed. And washed..."

"Jenny!?" I said.

"She hasn't spoken in three years!"

"She talked to me."

"What!?"

"Yeah! We booked her out and took her up to Su's. She was talking then. And she knew what to do. I mean, she walked out to the car like she'd been doing it every day of her life."

"Arnold!" Ern whispered. "It's a miracle."

"Aw, come on," I said. "I don't do miracles. And you don't believe in them."

"Listen," she said. "I heard all about Jenny from Su. And I know. Up till a week or two ago anyway, she never said a word."

I thought back to the way she was when we left for the Meads, and I could believe it. From the day Farmer hit her and Johnny lifted her off the ground, she never knew a thing. If it hadn't been for Johnny and that way he had that he learned from Su, she'd have died in the first month when we were all still up to Wooji.

"I was surprised to see her sitting in the window," I said. "Expected her to be still in bed, I guess. But there she was."

"She woke up one night a few months after you left," Ern told me, "and since then she's been able to get up every day. But as for talking... Not one word!"

I was so amazed by all Ern was telling me I didn't notice a thing I ate. Didn't even notice I was eating till my plate was empty and I was still hungry.

"Are you sure she's better?" Ern asked me then.

"Yes," I said. "She's better."

"And are you really taking her? Up the mountains?"

"Yes."

"Then I'll give in my notice in the morning."

I guess my jaw dropped.

"You'll be needing me," she said. "Jenny may be better, but she's been as good as dead for three years. She'll need a woman."

"You'll come?" I choked. "But..."

"I've had it in the back of my mind for awhile," she said. "You know that bald-headed guy I've been steering clear of. Well, he's an agent. Somebody wants to buy the house. There's a rumour they're planning another arcade. And I guess it's time."

"But when you come back..."

"Maybe I won't come back. It's not the same. And if you're staying up... I've been thinking, maybe I could take my share of the money and buy a flower shop. Or maybe a market garden. What do you think?"

Red Dragon Square

Part 2

*"...the hay is withered away, the
grass faileth, there is no green thing."*
(Isaiah 15:6)

Chapter: 1

I could see it was my own fault. I mean, nobody else invited Su up the Meads, I promised Jenny she could leave the hospital, got steam-rollered by Ern's peculiar logic. When I left the Meads, if I saw Ern and found Missy I'd have thought I'd done everything needful. But next morning I'm on the bus for Hawberry, going up to see George and arrange the trip back.

George would be surprised. But Sindabardi Bus Lines, in my experience, were never overbooked. Well, there was no shortage of seats till we got well down, past Hill City. And George didn't see any problem about waiting till I was ready to start back.

No, passengers wouldn't be a problem. Not going up, for sure. But baggage might. Didn't want too much weight. Sindabardi hadn't bought a new vehicle since about the time I was born, when they acquired the present fleet of one, at third or fourth hand then, and I was a bit concerned.

Travelling up the delta that morning I should have been looking forward, taking stock. But as the flats went by... factories, dorm towns, farmland... my mind travelled back.

Three years.

The bridge was out at Hawberry.

Johnny and I stood on the canal bank where the road ended.

Down in the ditch some chocolate-coloured sludge that passed for water was oozing over what was left of the bridge.

Nobody around. Apart from the dry grass, there wasn't a living thing but a bird high up in the sky.

After we looked awhile without saying much, we went back to the empty street and sat out front of a boarded-up tavern. That was where we left Johnny's car. Funny, Su offered me that car for my visit this time. Must have got it back somehow. Said she had her ways.

Well, after a few minutes sitting there, this shadow falls across our feet and somebody says, "The bridge is out."

I swear my hair stood on end. I mean, there beside us, standing with his back to the light, was somebody that materialized out of thin air.

"Used to be traffic here," he says. "Before the marshes silted up. Before the flood of sixty-eight, that would be. No way up-country now though. Only the barges on the dredging streams. Nothing but barges nowadays, and them a long way off."

Johnny had his legs stretched out and his hands shoved in his pockets. Never took his eyes off the grass across the canal. Miles and miles of it before you came to a purple smudge that I figured was probably foothills.

Neither of us spoke.

"Lost your way, have you?" the stranger says.

"No," Johnny says after awhile. "No, we're not lost. We're making for the Moonstream Gap."

"Oh," the stranger says. "The Moonstream Gap. 'Away over the Moonstream, the fair and farther Moonstream."

Johnny looked at him then! Recognized the words or something, I guess. "Only we can't fly," he said.

"Not as the bird flies, no," the stranger says. "No man has wings. But we fly by nature too. Try old Maggie Hyslop now. Might be she can help."

"Got a broomstick, has she?" I muttered.

"No, no. Nothing like that in these parts," he says, like he's taking me seriously. "Maggie used to run a millrace down the water, and the flying fox is still intact."

Johnny stood up like he was going to start out right away.

"Only thing is," the stranger says, "before you can fly, you must walk. Above five miles, I reckon, with the sun at your back."

"No carriage but my own two feet. No shelter but my skin," Johnny says, and looks straight at him.

I still couldn't see the features, but I saw the head nod. And I heard the laugh in the voice as the stranger said, "I have very good eyesight. Most people wouldn't believe..."

I understood just enough to know that I was missing something.

I looked from one to the other and back again, without becoming any wiser, and gave it up when Johnny set off along a path of packed earth between the ditch on one side and high, dry grass on the other. Thought I might as well tag along. Didn't expect much to come of it, and didn't think highly of a walk of five miles either. But I'd come this far. Might as well see it through.

After awhile some bleached buildings loomed up in the distance. And a mile or two after that we could make out this old person on a bench against the side of a barn.

"We've come to take the fox," Johnny says, when we finally came up to her.

She eyed us up and down.

"Hm-m," she says, looking at me. "I wonder now, dearie. Will the old fox carry you these days? She's pretty old and rotten. Might dump you half way over."

"I'll go first then," Johnny tells me, with a big grin.

Then he turns to Maggie.

"I'm going over," he says, "and I understand your fox is the only way across."

That was all there was to it. Not, "We're going over,"or "We're looking for a way," just "I'm going over."

"Very likely," the old woman says. "But we'll have to think on this."

That made sense to me. "I'll take a look at the mechanism if you don't mind," I said.

"Help yourself, my dear," she told me. "Nothing like a satisfied customer... Or a wise man!"

She looked at me like she was really seeing me when she said that, and I
had sense enough to wonder if I was, a wise man. Figured I probably wasn't, but
knew I still had the option if I wanted to take it.

Turned away and went into the dark mill. The sun was sinking over the
marsh and reddening, and there was just enough light left. Wouldn't last long.

Found the fox and looked her over. Figured she'd do. Hammered a few
joints here and there, testing strength, and when I came out, the sun was
disappearing into a lagoon of purple mist, and Maggie was coming toward me.

"Come along then," she says. "There's pancakes and honey and a cup of
tea. Not fare for a fine young prince, but good and filling."

That was the first time I heard Johnny called a prince.

"Don't know about his majesty there," I said, "but I'm hungry. Pancakes
sound good."

She looked at me like I said something disrespectful, even dangerous, but
she led the way to a lean-to kitchen where she had the table set. Seemed pleased to
have us. Sang all the time she cooked for us, songs I sort of remembered from
somewhere.

That night we slept on piles of dry grass in the barn and I thought I still
heard singing. Children singing. "Can't go around it, have to go up it... Can't go
up it, have to go over it... Can't go over it..."

Johnny was always singing bits of that song.

Dreaming! All those children had black curls and blue eyes! Lord! A
world of Johnnys!

Next time I woke, the sun was coming through the cracks in the barn and
Maggie was standing in the doorway.

"What will you give me if I put you over there?" she asked.

Johnny sat up. "I'll give you my white silk shirt," he said. "And I'll
throw in the slacks if you find us marsh boots. We didn't come prepared for
walking in the grass."

Her eyes shone. "Done!" she cried. "Come sit you down and take your
breakfast like the fine young prince you are, and Meg will come again."

It surprised me that Johnny took all this prince stuff without batting an eye, but I kept my mouth shut. I'd find a time to ask him. Besides, I had more important things on my mind. "You're not really going over there!" I said.

He looked surprised.

"I mean, we aren't prepared!"

"I am," he said.

"Aw, come on! It's five hundred miles over that blasted grassland, and we didn't even bring a chocolate bar! Besides, there's your car to think of."

"There's nothing to think of," he says, "but finding the Moonstream Gap. I'll have what I need. You can take the car back to town if you want to. Tell Su I gave it to you."

"Thanks a lot!" I said. "What if one of the things you need turns out to be me? Did you think of that?"

"Yes," he said. "If I need you, you'll come."

"Lord love us!" I grumbled. "Your majesty is bloody exasperating this morning!"

He grinned. "Princes are addressed as 'Highness,'" he said. "Your Highness."

"Blow highness!" I told him, but I don't think he heard me because Meg showed up just then with a bundle of boots and other stuff she thought we'd need. Some for me, some for Johnny.

"Meg thinks you're coming with me," he says.

"Look," I said, trying again, "we can't take the car over. That's clear. And bargees don't take passengers. Not going up at least. Coming down they may— for a price. But I mean, do we have to walk? There must be some way!"

"Suit yourself," he says.

He knew damn well I wouldn't. Even old Meg knew that! And it was no surprise to anybody that we were both across the canal and looking back from a knoll half a mile away while the morning was still getting started.

It was hot and humid even at that hour, and being in no very cheerful mood wasn't helping any.

Meg was there in the distance, waving her old red table cloth to catch our eye— and her wearing Johnny's white silk clothes, that stood out for fifty miles around! But I only snorted.

Johnny capered around and waved both arms above his head. Seemed happy— happier than I'd seen him for a long time.

"This is more like it!" he says, as he starts off again.

"Damn fool!" I growled to myself.

Felt like giving him my opinion half a dozen times, but decided not to have anything to say at all. Being no marshie-boy, the trek alone, that I let myself in for, would have made me snarl if I opened my mouth, so I kept quiet.

It was late summer, and the ground was mostly dry and hard. Grass was dead and brown. Big green patches still steamed where the land was low, but it was easy enough to get around them. Weren't even many insects. That was a good thing too— the ones that were there bit like hell!

Wasn't near as bad as it might have been, and that made me even crankier! Couldn't find enough complaints to satisfy me! Seems pretty stupid, looking back, but nobody's perfect.

After a few miles, though, my pack began to rub one shoulder and give me a real reason to grumble. But I made a pad of a pair of socks and carried on. It was already too late to turn back. And I knew I wouldn't do it if I could.

Johnny marched on without looking around.

"Be damned to you, then," I muttered.

Made no effort to catch up. Knew I couldn't lose him. I mean, a blind man could see forever across those crawling marshes, which was partly what was bothering me. Being used to the City or the hills, I hate flat, open places.

Then, around mid-morning, the sun cleared the sky from pale purple to blue and started in on me. My mouth went dry and my lips cracked...

The bus swerved to miss a man on a bicycle and I came to with a start and a dry mouth. No signs of arriving anywhere, though. Hoped it wouldn't be too long. Moved across the aisle to the shady side and looked out the window at that never-ending grass...

The old mill was almost lost in the shimmer of heat haze on the horizon. I took off my hat and wiped the sweatband dry. Felt like a beetle holding up the weight of the sky.

But in the next dry watercourse, a big tree stump reared out of a pan of silt and made a patch of shadow on the ground. It was knee-deep in soft earth, a great place for bugs and birds. But good for a man to rest out of the heat of the day too.

Johnny was already hunkered down when I got there, and he passed me the jug of water Maggie gave us.

"Worth more than a silk shirt any day," he said, and leaned back against the stump.

I didn't say anything. Just scowled at a black and orange butterfly that fluttered onto a gandle pod and hung there. Wouldn't even admit to myself the thing was pretty. Watched it, though, till my back relaxed against the stump and my eyes closed...

Just as I did that day on the marsh, I relaxed against the seat in the bus and dropped off.

I thought Missy was coming. I was just turning my head to see her, when I woke with my heart pounding like the wheels of the bus, that was still purring up the delta.

For a minute I didn't know where I was and started to my feet, but I made it look like I was just shifting position and none of the passengers noticed. They were all mostly half asleep anyway...

Johnny was on his feet yelling. Sweat poured down his back and hands. His eyes stared.

I wasn't surprised. We'd been through that before. But I figured, out there on the marsh, with nobody to hit and nothing to drink, he'd maybe have to come to grips with his dreams, so I left him alone. Besides, I still couldn't be bothered.

After a few minutes he picked up his pack and moved out. And I followed.

Two or three hours later, when a steady ache was settling in my hips and shoulders, we came to the top of a low rise. A breeze licked the sweat off my arms and legs and I shivered. God, what a forsaken place!

In every direction the marsh moved and rustled. Never stopped. Made me dizzy to look at it. But we'd been coming steadily onto higher ground, even though the blue smudge on the horizon wasn't even a shade broader.

We sat down together there and ate some bread and drank some water. It was hot on the ground, out of the breeze, and the light glinted. But if you kept your hat low over your eyes you could break the glare, and the rest felt good.

Still weren't talking though. Johnny was suffering the effects of the dream and I was sticking to my policy of non-interference. That's what I called it! We needed something to make us laugh, but we weren't finding it.

Starting out again, the slope was more noticeable, and the ground was covered with a low plant that caught our feet and sank sharp thorns into our legs. After a while the scratches itched and burned.

By mid-afternoon the country was rolling and the rustling seemed worse. My breath rasped in my throat, and my eyes ached from the constant shimmer. All I was doing then was just keeping my head down, lifting one foot past the other, and wondering how long before my legs gave it up altogether. We'd covered miles but didn't seem to be getting anywhere. And then, as the sun started to sink, I started worrying about shelter for the night.

Not watching where I was going, I missed my footing and fell, and a bunch of big, blue flies swarmed out of the grass. Found a few words to say about that! But stayed where I was for a minute or two and the rest did me good. Felt better when I got up and pushed on to the spot where Johnny disappeared into the next dip.

From up there the marsh looked rough. Pitted with depressions like the one I fell in. Dried pools, I guess. Some full of tangled plants, some paved with sun-cracked silt.

One of the bare patches would have to do us for the night, I figured, but there was still some light and the flies still bit behind my knees, so I struggled on, trying to keep Johnny in sight. The last thing I wanted then, with the land rolling more and more and dark coming on, was to lose him altogether.

Pretty soon the light and I were just about done. I didn't know whether to put on one last spurt and catch up or fall down where I was and to hell with him, when out of the corner of my eye I saw this short stake sticking out of the silt at the edge of a dry pan. Beside it, half buried in the mud, was this length of cord.

"Frog traps," I muttered. "Somebody's been catching mud frogs."

Don't know how I knew. Must have heard it somewhere. But the idea that somebody else had ever been in that creeping place made me feel better.

I looked at the stake, trying to take it in, and noticed what seemed like a faint path leading away from it.

Johnny was out of sight again, but following that path, before long I saw him up ahead just coming to a weatherbeaten cabin. Hadn't seen human habitation for a good long time, and to a city boy that shanty felt like coming home. I could have cheered— if I hadn't been so dry....

The bus was slowing down. It rolled past two or three shacks not unlike the one on the marsh and drew up in front of a general store. Comfort stop. Drinks. Sandwiches. And not before time.

Walking up and down beside the bus, drinking something cold and enjoying the breeze off the marsh, I thought what a city boy I must have been three years ago. Couldn't understand, at the time, why Johnny wasn't stopping at the first cabin we came to, and I could have killed him if he'd been near enough to get my hands on him...

Just there the path became almost a road. It turned eastward, out of our way, and ran up toward the sky where one or two stars were coming out; but any road would have looked good to me then.

I hurried up the rise to get a look at the country round about before final dark, and in the distance, far off but real enough, light glowed.

I collapsed on the ground and nearly cried. Lamplight. Coming from a window. House, barn, or woodshed, didn't matter to me; I was looking at a window with light in it! And there was water just beyond. Free, running water, it looked like. A barge canal most likely.

Thank God!

But I had to rest a minute...

The rest out of the bus felt good, but I ate a baloney sandwich, which didn't sit too well. Could have been that. Or could have been remembering the knot in my stomach when I heard the noise spilling out of that canalden...

Johnny was inside and in a mess of trouble. That was clear. I figured I better get rid of my pack and find something to grip in my hand before I went in there. Bargees, every one of them. And big!

I was in time to hear the biggest one say, "Speak up, gendy. We don't want you here, and we're gonna run you off, but first you're gonna tell us what you know."

"I keep telling you I have nothing to do with the law," Johnny says, real patient.

"Think I don't know gendy when I see it?" this goon snarls.

Then he lunges, but Johnny dodges around a sideboard and grabs a bottle off a shelf.

The rest of them laugh and cheer the big guy on. "Go, Dobby!" they say. "Give it to him, Dobby!" "He's no match for you, Dob!"

Johnny held the bottle by the neck.

"I'm not the law," he said. "I have nothing to do with the City."

"For God's sake!" Dobby snorts. "Expect me to believe that? Stinking gendy, I can smell you! And I'll see you in the quickmud soon's I'll look at you. Speak up if you don't want me to spoil your baby-face to start with."

He lunged for Johnny's shoulder, but the bottle came down across his wrist and he swore.

I braced myself for what I knew would happen, and sure enough, Dobby turned away, half stumbling, clutching his wrist. Then he twisted around and kicked.

Johnny saw the move coming and turned so he took the blow on the thigh, but it threw him off balance and Dobby hit him across the neck. He fell, and another one of them kicked him on the side of the head as he hit the floor.

"Take him out and dump him," Dobby snarls.

Then he looks up and sees me standing in the doorway, just about filling it, with a pitchfork in my hands.

Didn't quite catch what he said then, but somebody down the back hollered, "There's another one! Clear out!"

And they scattered like a pack of rats!

I moved around to the water side and watched them swarming down the path and onto their barge. It was beautiful. That old black scow was out in clear water quicker than anything I ever saw in my life.

But I was worried about Johnny. So when I knew they were leaving, I walked into the den and found a skinny woman and a weedy old man lifting him off the floor.

The woman had his feet. The old man had him by the shoulders. And as they lifted, his head fell sideways, and the gold medallion he always wore on a chain inside his shirt slipped out and glinted in the lamplight.

"My God!" the woman whispered. "Is that what I think it is?"

She dropped his feet and snatched at the medallion.

"Look at it!" she cried. "It's real! They'll come, certain. Them highalt people knows, and this one's awful high. That there's one of the fancy kind."

The old man lowered Johnny's head and shoulders gently to the floor and bent over the medallion with her.

"I believe you're right," he said. "Highalt for sure. That's no gendy. That's a prince of the highalt!"

The prince business again.

Well, fine. I'd make use of it.

I stepped into the light. "What have you done to His Highness?" I said, real stern.

The two of them looked up at me with their mouths open.

Then the woman starts in to talk!

"Strangers!" she says. "Pon my soul. Where in the system did you drop from? We didn't hear you coming up the water."

"We came across the marsh," I said, as if it was really none of her business. "From a place called Hawberry."

"From Hawberry?" she squawked. "But there's no road."

"Road?" I said, like I didn't know what she meant and never used them.

Then I said, "I believe you were trying to carry His Highness to that couch across the room? We'll do that now and see to his injuries.

Johnny's skin looked gray and blood ran from one nostril, but his eyes opened and there was life in them.

The woman rushed to the kitchen for water and a clean cloth, and we wiped away the blood. Then I sent her and the old man for bandages and brandy. Anything to get them out of the way.

"Are you all right?" I whispered, when they were gone.

He grabbed my arm. "They were arguing back and forth," he croaked, "but you should have heard the silence when they saw me standing in their midst."

"Shut up," I said.

"No, but it was so funny!" he says. "The whole bunch of them! Frozen like I was a ghost or something."

"You almost were," I muttered.

The woman came running back with a bottle of something that smelled like disinfectant in her hand. I thought it was probably safe to use on cuts and bruises, and that shut him up for a while.

"They're not used to company," I told him. "Especially not company that comes to the back door."

"What is this place?"

"It's a canalden," I said. "Bargees lay up here for food and rest."

"Thought they must be bargees," he said. "There was this big one..."

"Keep your mouth shut," I said. "You can tell me later."

He seemed to catch on. At least he didn't say anything more while the den people were around.

I raised my voice. "Where's that brandy?"

The old man came scuttling from somewhere with another bottle. "Here, sir," he says. "Just coming. Knew I had it somewhere."

I poured a little into a cup and tasted it. Seemed all right, so I gave the prince a mouthful.

"Good stuff," he says. "Where...?"

"Shut up, Your Highness," I warned him. "Do as I tell you." I pushed him down on the couch and held him there.

"Now," I said to the den people. "That is stew I smell, is it not? I find I'm hungry after a day of much activity."

"Of course!" the woman said. "I'll get you some right away, sir."

"That's not the way you answered me when I asked for food," Johnny says.

"Now, now, lovey— Your Highness," she starts in. "Your poor head. It's all scrambled about. You're remembering things all wrong. I never..."

"Indeed!?" says Johnny, and it could have been Su herself lying there.

"Well, I mean, walking in from the marshes, Your Highness! How could we believe... We didn't know... I mean, we thought you were gendy— officer of the law, you know."

"Often get law officers here, do you?" I said.

"Oh, no, no," the old man says, real quick. "No, no. Nothing like that, sir. Law abiding in this den, we are. Swear to that. I knew His Highness there was no gendy. None of them ever came to the back door of no canalden I ever seen. Not in my... I mean, not to my knowledge, anyway. Not that they're not always trying something new, gendies. For all the good it does them! And where there's one..."

"Quite so," I said. "The man Dobby made it clear that where there is one trooper walking in there will be half a dozen more out in the nethermere."

"That was when the lady offered to give me stew in the middle of the mechcanal with a length of chain around my neck," Johnny put in.

The lady's mouth opened.

So did mine, to hiss, "Shut up, for God's sake!"

But Johnny knew what he was doing. "I believe my friend ordered a dish of stew?" he said.

The woman hurried to the kitchen without another word, and the old man after her.

"They were good, Arnold," Johnny whispered, and touched his head carefully. "Spread out like a team. Knew what they were doing."

"Yes, but the one called Dobby has the IQ of a mudshark," I said. "And a good thing for you too. Don't you know anything about the gendy?"

"Didn't think there was any reason to lie," he said.

"Didn't think at all," I snarled. "I'll think for both of us in this place."

He didn't argue but shut his eyes then and sort of slid away. Breathed regular though, and his colour was pretty good.

The den woman crept closer. "Poor lovey. Ain't he pretty," she said.

Even so, I spent the night in a chair with my feet on the end of the couch. Once I woke and heard the woman and the old man whispering in the kitchen, but they didn't come near and I dropped off again.

About daybreak they opened the door and stood looking out. I could tell by the sounds coming in that another barge was making fast to the dock, so I stretched myself and joined them.

While my back was turned, Johnny sat up. The noise must have wakened him too. He threw off his blanket and lowered his feet to the floor. First I knew of it, we heard this groan, and the woman and I ran and held him till he righted himself.

The woman wanted to put him back to bed, but he made us help him to the table in the middle of the room. For a minute I thought he was going to pass out again, but he rallied and asked for water.

I poured some brandy in a cup, as much to kill the residents as anything, then added water from a jug and gave it to him.

While I did that, the old man sat down opposite and watched us as the sounds of the barge arriving grew louder.

"Can't just bring to mind, I reckon," he suggested after a minute or two. "Can't just recall, now, how you come to have that lump on the side of the head, shouldn't wonder." And he closed one eye.

Johnny looked at him blankly.

"I mind once," the old man went on, rubbing his chin. "Forty... Fifty year ago. Fell from a yardarm. Couldn't call to mind how I done it... Oh, nigh on twenty year. Came back to me eventually, though."

"I dare say it will come back to me in time," Johnny said slowly.

The old man nodded. "Bound to. Bound to," he said. "But not too soon, I shouldn't wonder. Not too soon."

He got up and shuffled around the table to stand behind Johnny's chair and examine the swelling on his head. "You'll do," he said, and returned to the doorway.

Johnny forced himself to his feet and leaned against the table. I knew he was testing his legs and head, so I let him do it. He stood for a minute, then sat down again, very carefully, and took a sip of the brandy and water.

"I'm all right," he said. "Look after things."

I took that to mean he wanted me to keep an eye on the barge that was coming in, so I left him and went back to the door.

It was interesting. I'd never seen a barge work into a canalden before, coming in on underwater cables through the rushes. I'd always been on the barge, not the other way around. Not every day you see a barge like that either. I knew her type— big, heavy, and slow.

"Jody Ruddin," the woman said. "Heading upstream. He'll be no good to you. But he'll tell the first downie to stop in for you."

"We don't get downies here," the old man explained. "They run with the current and stay out in the stream. No sense to working all the way in here when they're making time on the water. It's when they're going against the stream they stop in the canaldens. Going up is when they're working hard."

He glanced at me out of the corner of his eye, but I didn't let on there wasn't much about barges that was news to me.

"How long will they stay?" I asked.

"Till the sun goes down," he said. "Dock mech gets too hot to handle during the day. They'll leave a couple of hours after sundown and be well on their way by moonrise."

"What kind of crew?"

Neither of them answered.

"His Highness is going upstream," I said, "and we'll take the first available transport, which is that barge out there. So what kind of people are they?"

The woman shrugged. "They're bargees," she said. "Bargees is bargees. You must be scrambled in the head too. They don't take passengers."

I gave her the cold stare. "They'll take us," I said.

"His Highness there is in no shape to travel on no black canalbarge," she howled.

But Jody Ruddin and his crew were coming ashore then, and they were through the door before they realized we were there.

You talk about surprised bargees! I could hardly keep a straight face. Only the thought that one of them might recognize me saved the situation. I mean, I never heard of Ruddin himself, but you never knew. One of his crew might have sat next to me in third grade! Luckily they were all strangers.

The old man giggled into the silence, and the woman's tongue started up again.

"Meet our stray waif," she said. "Found him on the path to the frog ponds with a lump on his head big as a pawpye's egg, and no notion who he was or where he come from. Brought him home and kind of took to him. Then his friend here showed up looking for him."

The bargees grunted but didn't move.

Johnny rose to his feet, easier this time. "We're going up-country," he said. "We'll leave with you this evening."

"Ho!" says Jody Ruddin.

That was the only sound.

"Where are you assigned?" I asked.

"Canalhead."

"Canalhead!" the old man says. "Naw, Canalhead. End of the world. You don't want to go to Canalhead, Your Highness! Away to hell up the water? Head of the mechcanal! Take six, seven days from here, way the water is— if the lily eels and mudshells hasn't fouled the cables, which as like as not they have! And judging by the way that there barge sets in the water, she's heavy laden. I'll put you at ten days from here. That's if the water holds..."

I figured the old fellow didn't often get a silence to fill all by himself. Knew somebody would take a hand pretty soon. But it wasn't up to his lordship's companion, so I looked on and enjoyed the show.

Johnny wasn't quite up to it either, so Ruddin got in the first word.

"Shut your gop, old man," he growled. "I'll do the talking. You know so much, you tell me how this feller here comes to think we'll take him. Him and his bodyguard. We don't run no Vanderanian pleasure scow."

The crew grinned and tittered.

"That barge out there is a black canal drudge," Jody rumbled. "Worth every credit in her makeup, but she'd kill a marshie-boy with a lump on the side of his head."

"That's right, lovey!" the woman cried. "You want to rest up and get over that clout you got alongside the head."

Johnny straightened himself. "No carriage but my own two feet. No shelter but my skin," he said, and walked toward the door.

I braced myself, but there was no more argument. The bargees parted and let him through.

He had just enough strength to walk out that door. I knew better than to try and help him, but I followed and was there to pick up the pieces and arrange them in a hammock under some cottonwood trees.

Through the walls of the den we listened to them arguing. Were we lawmen? Didn't look like lawmen. But not marshie-boys neither. A prince of the highalt, then? The old man held to that theory.

But Jody Ruddin laughed. "Ain't no such thing as the highalt," he hooted.

"Shh-h! He'll hear you!" the woman hissed.

"What about this prince business?" I said.

"For God's sake!" Johnny laughed, and closed his eyes.

Chapter: 2

Hawberry! End of the Line!" the driver called down the bus, and the passengers yawned and stretched. I helped a lady with a bunch of boxes and bags, and before I knew where I was, I was shivering on the boardwalk in front of the Hawberry Bar and Grill.

Couldn't get over Hawberry. Missed it on the way down because of arriving after dark and leaving again before daylight. Walked along noticing everything. Not much like three years back!— except that the marsh was bleached and yellow like it was then.

Strolled to the end of the boardwalk, which was also the end of town, and stood looking northward. Over the new bridge. Over the near meadows. Over those miles of waving grass to the thin purple smudge at the end of the world.

Canalhead was somewhere up in there.

My stomach knotted again, but I knew what it was this time— if I wanted to. The thing was, I didn't want to. Not yet. So I walked back the way I came, noticing every new lick of paint and pane of glass along the street and keeping an eye out for George— first turn past the bus stop, in the alley behind the hardware store. Found him tinkering with the old engine and whistling between his teeth.

"Thought you might be along today," he said. "Ready to start back?"

"Not quite. Soon. You?"

"Yeah. For myself, I've had enough of these crawling marshes," he said. "But we have a problem."

"The carburettor?"

"Worse than that. She needs a proper burial. She'll maybe get us across the grassland, but we'll walk most of the way up hill."

"That would take you the best part of five years," I said.

"Don't laugh," he told me.

I wasn't laughing.

"Now if we only had some money," he said, "there's this sweet little van for sale around the corner. I could kiss Sindabardi Bus Lines good-bye and go into business for myself. She's big enough for up the Meads. And you talk about power! And handling! With a little adjustment for altitude... Mate, I'd be sitting pretty."

He sighed.

"But," he said, "no use dreaming. You lay in a supply of rubber bands and we'll do the best we can."

"George," I said, "let's have the truth. I mean, how much of this makes a good story and how much is real bad news?"

"I will not lie to you, Arnold," he said. "I don't see this old bus making it back past Canalhead— if you're still planning on going in there? She might have a few years left as a burger bus down the corner."

"Then let's go and look at the van."

"What!?" he hollers.

"Let us," I said. "Go. And look at. The van."

"You're kidding!"

"No."

"You got the credits?"

I nodded.

"Arnold!" he whispers. "Partner! Buddy! You won't be sorry! But let me do the talking."

So half an hour later we had exchanged Sindabardi's old bus and a considerable amount of Johnny's credit for an almost new van, white with red seats, tinted glass, and what George assured me was the sweetest little motor in any ten states.

Not wanting to appear too eager, we left the van where it was and went to celebrate over lunch in the Hawberry Hotel. But George could hardly sit still for dreaming about becoming an entrepreneur with his own bus line.

"What'll we call her?" he says. "George & Co.? Or would you money-bags like your names on too? Doyle, Grieve, and..."

"George & Co.," I said. "You get the name painted on and buy a luggage trailer and be ready to start in four or five days' time."

"No problem. No problem," he says. "Been doing some shopping, have you?"

"George," I said, "prepare yourself. I do not come alone."

His eyes gleamed. "Paying passengers?"

"Sorry," I said. "All family. My sister. Jenny. And— I am very much afraid— Johnny's mother."

"You are very much afraid."

"Very much."

"Oh, well," he says. "Have to take the bitter with the sweet. Be going right up the Meads, will she?"

"Right up the Meads."

Then he caught on and laughed. "Why do I kind of figure Johnny's a little like her?" he says.

"A lot like her," I agreed, with a big grin.

"Then I'll look forward to meeting the lady," he says. "Maybe she'll make the Meads the fashion and we'll need a fleet."

"Lord love us, I hope not," I thought, as I bit into a thick mutton sandwich.

George itched to take possession of the van and start greasing and washing and polishing— not to mention getting 'George & Co.' painted on the doors. Rambled on about what he had to do, what he'd have to do, what he'd like to do if... Did I think..?

"Sure," I said. "Anything in reason."

Then to cool off from the fires in his eyes I leaned back and let everything roll over me— Hawberry, the bridge, the sea of grass....

The marsh was dark and cool when we went aboard Jody Ruddin's barge.

They threw down a couple of sleeping bags for us, and Johnny fell asleep as soon as he stretched out. But I laid awake a long time watching the stars and listening to the sounds of the barge and the water. Seemed like they should be telling me something.

In the morning we were still travelling steadily northward through tall grass. Except where they had cut passing bays into the bank every few miles, the channel was narrow. Sometimes, looking ahead, you'd swear it was too narrow for the barge to pass through. Right where you were, though, there was always lots of water.

"What are those big holes in the bank every now and then?" Johnny says to me.

"Why ask me?" I say.

"Sorry," he says. "You don't know about barges, do you."

So he asks Jody.

"Passing bays," Jody says.

Johnny is no wiser.

"Downstream barges has the right of way," Jody tells him, speaking like he thinks maybe that lump on the side of the head is making Johnny a little slow on the uptake. "When we know somebody's coming down," he says, "we'll work into a passing bay and wait him by."

He rolled away forward then, but a young fellow— looked about fifteen— opened up to us. "Jody's a good barge master," he said. "Knows by the sound of the cable when a meet is coming and never has to move stern first— back up, I mean."

We both nodded.

"Old Tillie Vetchcum met us coming down the other week and had to back up half a tencab," this young fellow tells us. "Then she couldn't make the back connection and had to slide on by and bring her in head first. You should have heard us laugh and cheer!"

Johnny was getting lost in the details again, but trying to look like he understood. Me, I was trying to look like I didn't!

"Jody wouldn't let us sluice her down, though," the kid says. "Jody's a fair man. The very best. We been running up to Canalhead for eighteen months now and never had a stern meet yet."

"What's in the cargo?" Johnny says.

I held my breath, knowing what a sensitive question that could be, bargees being bargees. But the kid looks him straight in the eye like he never even heard of contraband and says, "Stuff for the mine at Jumper Hill— machines and that. And general cargo for Canalhead."

Looked like he was telling the truth. Maybe he was— as far as he knew it. Who was I to judge?

Johnny nodded— he understood mining. And I was satisfied as far as the story went, but I figured there had to be more to it. Pure acrite going back up, maybe. Weapons, perhaps. Something was making the run pay...

Came to, alone at the hotel table, wondering how I could've been so casual in those days. I mean, guns? Acrite? Just like they didn't matter?

Walked out along the canal to clear my head. Walked till I thought I should be able to see old Meg's mill in the distance. But nothing. Gone. Only the marsh as far as the eye could see. No need for the flying fox now the bridge was up again. Funny the way things turn out.

Came back and sat in the garden behind the Old Mill Hotel with a jug of jilly in front of me and time on my hands. Something about that garden reminded me of my house up the Meads, and I felt content. Maybe it was the roses growing over the door to the bar, I don't know, but I felt warm and settled. The marsh uneasiness wasn't as bad in there. I could almost believe...

"It is!" a child's voice whispered.

"No. It can't be!"

"It is, Daddy. It's him!"

There was nobody else in the garden. They must be whispering about me. But that contented feeling kept me from looking around.

Pretty soon small feet sneaked up behind me. I felt breath on my neck.

Then a strand of long red hair fell across my shoulder.

"Maudy!" I hollered.

"It's him! It's him! It's him!" she screeched.

I caught her in a big one-armed hug— one-armed because the other hand was grabbed by one of the best people Johnny and I ever met..

Well, Budd and I laughed and pounded each other, and Maudy went streaking into the hotel for her mother, and we were soon all around my little table, all talking at once, and me holding Maudy on my lap and squeezing her every now and then.

"Where's Johnny?" she kept whispering. "Where's Johnny, Arnold? Did He?"

"You too, Maudy?" I said with a sigh. "None of the girls can see me for looking for Johnny. He isn't here, love."

"No, but did He?"

"Did he what, Maudy?" Alice asked in that quiet way she always has with the kids.

"Don't you remember, Mother?" Maudy cried. "You said God should go with him, and the light shined. So did He, Arnold?"

"Yes, Maudy," I said slowly. "I think He did."

She was delighted.

But Maudy is a practical little soul too. "And did you eat my lunch?" she asked.

"Yes, and you'll never guess who helped us," I teased.

"Who?"

"This beautiful cat, Maudy. This great big, gorgeous cat, called Oomiskaya. Peanut butter sandwiches are his favourite food. He wants them every day. We're trying to grow peanuts up the Meads so he can have them."

Maudy's eyes danced. "Tell me everything about him," she cried.

"That would take a long time," I laughed, "and I have to catch the bus back to town in an hour."

"Oh, do you have to?" she cried. "You could stay with us. Couldn't he, Mother?"

"Of course. Any time..."

But, "Alice!" somebody called from the bar.

"Coming," she said, and hurried away.

"You'll have to come back and stay with us some day when Alice is off work and the boys are home," Budd said. "The kids are helping a fellow cut grass this afternoon. Bobby wants to earn enough to buy a few chooks."

He laughed, but he looked thin and older, tired.

"What are you doing here?" I said, as if I didn't notice. "This is about the last place..."

"The work and the old truck ran out about the same time," he said. "I was hauling slabs of that pink rock from Penner's for awhile, and then marble from the Bar. Good times while they were building Gihon Square. Boom ended a few months back."

"Hawberry looks booming enough still," I said.

"All on the surface, Arnold," he told me. "The paint is still new, so hard times don't show yet. But they will before long. Already Alice is afraid of losing her job in the hotel."

"And you don't think of going back to Hill City?"

"Sold the place there," he said. "You know what it's like. No place for kids."

I nodded.

"Always thought of staying up the Hellish," he said, like he was talking of a dream. "Probably told you that. But nobody's up there now. Which is even worse for kids. Need a school, and friends to grow up with."

"Know anything about growing peanuts?" I asked, to get him going.

"No," he said, with his old good-humoured grin. "No. Trained as a cabinet maker, though, in my youth. A long time ago. If you know of anybody needs a hard worker that can choose a tree and see it through till it's a table or a chair— none of this junk!"

He kicked at one of the hotel's plastic chairs and turned it over. Got up at once to right it, though— that would be Budd.

"Be ready to leave for Medalsring in four or five days," I said. "We're rebuilding the village. Need you the worst way."

Maudy was listening, hardly breathing.

She slid off my knee then and put her hand on his arm. "Can we, Daddy?" she whispered.

He smiled and stroked her hair. "Would you like to, honey?" he asked her.

"Could Bobby have some chooks?" she said, looking at me.

"All he wants," I said.

"And could we go to school?"

"I'll be bringing the teacher with me."

Budd slapped the arm of his plastic chair, and he was the old Budd we knew again. "Alice!" he bellowed.

She appeared behind the screen door.

"Give in your notice, darlin'," he roared. "We're going home."

Alice came out then, wiping her hands on her apron the way I'd seen her do a thousand times.

"You mean it, Budd?" she whispered. "We're going home? Back to Hill City?"

I was on my feet then.

"Better than Hill City, Alice," I told her, and kissed her cheek. "Budd will explain, and we'll have the whole trip to fill in the details. Now, if I don't get out of here, I'll miss the bus. Look for George & Co."

Hurrying out to the street, I began to think, "How many will the van hold? There'll be George. Budd and me— we'll do some of the driving. Then we'll have Jenny, Ern, and Su. That's six already. And Alice and the three kids. Then if Missy..."

All right. It was time to face up to it. If Missy... If Missy what? The thing was, if. If Missy...

No, I couldn't do it yet. Missy was still two weeks away.

But my stomach felt better.

So, as the early winter dusk came on, I laid back in the bus and went to sleep. The last thing I remember seeing, just as I'm dropping off, is Johnny up the Meads. He's sitting with his feet dangling over the lip of the cirque. There's a fishing pole in his hand, and a long line stretching down the cliff. Every now and then he lifts the pole and pulls somebody up... Jenny... Su... Budd... Bobby...

Back in Red Dragon Square, when I walked up the alley, every light in the house was on and Ern was standing in the middle of the kitchen with a pot in one hand, a frying pan in the other, and her hair standing on end.

"What are you doing!?" I hollered.

"Well, I never moved before," she said, "and I've got a lot of stuff."

"Oh, no!" I said. "Not at this time of night."

I took the pot and pan out of her hands and put them away. Then I put her in a chair by the table and smoothed her hair.

"I'm hungry," I said. "Haven't eaten since lunch in Hawberry. You probably haven't eaten either. So I'll get out the bread and whatever, and you sit there and tell me what you think you're doing."

"Well," she said, "first thing today I dropped into the office and gave my notice. That floored them. Didn't think they'd ever get rid of me! But they were real nice about it. Thought I was crazy, of course, but didn't say so.

"Then I called the estate agent and he's coming noon tomorrow, when you're here. And I got an appraiser to come this afternoon and he promised we'd have his report by ten in the morning.

"And after that I went shopping.

"And then I started to pack."

I could see that!

"But I don't know how to do it, Arnold," she wailed. "You'll have to help me."

"Here," I said. "Have a sandwich. I'll do the packing. You can't bring everything in the house, you know. I haven't seen so much cargo since we went aboard Jody Ruddin's barge!"

"Jody Ruddin!" she whispers, with her eyes big and round. "I knew him! He died on the water. Did you know that?"

"I knew, Ern," I said, but I wasn't thinking about that. I was still stunned by her first attempt at packing.

"They found two barges," she said. "But none of the crew. Not one of the crew was ever seen again."

That stopped me. Though at the time...

But Ern was still talking. "Aren't we going by bus?" she was saying. "I thought that's what you told me. And there's only the four of us."

"Ern," I said, "I don't know where this thing is going to end. I feel like I'm collecting..."

Then I grabbed my hair and stirred it up. "Cranky!" I howled. "I forgot Cranky. He's got to come. And if Cally still has Buster..."

Ern grabbed her hair and mussed it up again. "I've got to make some sense of this!" she yelled. "Who's Buster?"

"Buster's a mongrel pup," I said. "He was half grown when I knew him. By now he'll be as big as..."

Ern reached out and smoothed my hair. "And who's Cally?" she said.

I looked at her for a minute. "Have you started in on the front room yet?" I asked.

She shook her head.

"Then we'll take our supper in there. You look like you won't get to sleep tonight, and I slept most of the way down in the bus."

"And about time," she muttered.

I knew she wasn't talking about sleeping. But once we were settled in the front room with the worst of the electric glare turned off, it wasn't easy to start.

"Ern," I said, "we were..."

"Yes. Go on."

"Well..."

"Go on, Arnold," she said, in that tone she used to use when she thought she had to be mothering me. "You've started just fine," she said. "Now keep on going."

So I took a deep breath.

"You ever seen empty docks, Ern?" I asked. "I never did before. Totally, absolutely empty. Tillie Vetchcum would have been the last to leave, and there wouldn't be another barge in till Dobby made it up the last lengths— which couldn't be too long for me!

"We left the canoe in an empty slip and went ashore as the sun was going down behind a spur of the dyke. Nobody met us, only this mongrel pup with a hungry look and his tail full of burrs."

"Is he important?"

"Yes, he's Buster."

"Oh. All right, then. Carry on."

"Well, Ern," I said, "Canalhead— what there is of it— is just this dusty square stretching back from the main slip with the first rise of the foothills behind it. At the top there's the Hotel Marshlands facing the water— three floors, painted rocking chairs on the verandah. You know. You've seen pictures."

"Dozens of them!"

"On either side there's a line of weatherbeaten shops and warehouses. That's all. Of course, everything was locked and bolted when we got there."

"Quiet sort of place," Johnny says. "Guess they weren't expecting us. Let's try The Marshlands."

I could have told him what would happen there, but I followed along and was right behind him when the manager looks him up and down and says, "I think you gentlemen would be more comfortable in the campground. Or Mrs. Presking might possibly take you— if you can pay cash..."

"He said that to Johnny!?" Ern gasped...

"Let's not embarrass the good folks at The Marshlands," I said. "And as I gather Mrs. Presking's policy is strictly cash and carry, we'll betake ourselves to the campground..."

"I thought some of Johnny was rubbing off on you!" Ern muttered. "So it was starting way back then..."

"Come on," I said. "They don't want us here. There'll be a store at the campground where we can get something to eat."

Well, Johnny followed me for a change, and pretty soon I found a rough track leading eastward out of the town between the Business Bank and a neat little house with a brass plaque on the door that said "Mrs. Martha Presking: Bargemen Boarded."

The track led us through a dump— rusty cans, broken bottles— then along a gully with a boardwalk squelching in thick mud. And from there up a sharpish climb to a narrow ridge.

A breeze was blowing across the ridge, and we stopped by a twisted old pine to look back at the town. Nice old tree, surviving somehow— reminded me of the old flame tree back in Red Dragon Square.

A light came on in Mrs. Presking's kitchen, but no use asking there.

In the other direction, straight over the ridge from the town, the campground spread out around two small lakes in a shallow bowl. It looked like every inch of ground had a tent on it, and the whole place was thick with the smoke of fires.

Johnny stared at the camp astounded. "Who's in all those tents!" he says.

"Passengers," I tell him. "I thought you knew."

I lowered my pack and the grub bag to the ground and sat down on a rock.

"This is Canalhead," I said. "One of them— there's others. At Canalheads the passengers come down. If they're rich enough— or look rich enough— they stay at The Marshlands— or The Imperial, or The Royal— whatever. Some, here, maybe stay at Ma Presking's, though she advertises for bargees and probably won't take passies. The rest stay at the campground. And when a barge comes in, they all try to buy passage to the City— or most of them do."

"But I thought the bargees didn't take passengers," Johnny says. "Didn't seem to want to take us."

"They don't," I said. "Not officially. But if somebody has lots of money— or something else valuable— why not unofficially? Jody never took passengers much, I guess, but you must have heard remarks about passies on the barge."

"I thought they were aimed at us," he said.

"Not entirely," I told him. "Jody'd take a few now and then. Dobby, now, he takes them sure. Most of his probably never reach the City, of course— die, get killed in a fight, fall overboard. Who's to know?"

Johnny was very quiet for awhile. "I never knew it was that bad," he said then. "There must be hundreds in the campground."

"It's hard to get farther down from Canalheads," I said. "Lots make it easy by other routes, but the ones that end up in campgrounds... Well, I guess the graveyard is over back somewhere."

Johnny looked at me like he thought I was making it all up— or hoped I was.

"Some passies been here for years," I said. "Set up in business selling supplies to other passies. Food, booze, tents, fire wood— stuff like that. Lots of people been born and raised in campgrounds."

"I never knew," he said, as if it mattered to him.

"Come on," I said. "There'll be a store down there. They'll charge us an arm and a leg, but they won't set the dogs on us. I have enough cash to pay for what we need."

Johnny shook himself. "Speaking of dogs," he says.

The pup was sitting just out of arm's reach. When he knew we were talking about him, he sidled up and thumped his tail against Johnny's leg.

"Better go home, fellah," Johnny says, but the mutt settles down at his feet instead and watches him with these big, adoring eyes.

"After we've bought some supplies," I said, "we'll have to go around the far side and try and find a place to sleep."

"Then let's go," Johnny says. "I could eat a horse— or a small brown dog!"

He took a friendly swipe at the pup, which Buster received as a sign of life-long approval. At least he tagged right along after us and stayed till we settled down in a dry place at the head of a little gully where a few bushes were growing against a rocky bank.

The sun was still warming the ground up there, but most of the camp below was already in shadow.

Didn't stop to make a fire. Too hungry. Just ate dry bread and cheese and some apples we bought, and drank a bottle of lukewarm water. Best supper I ever ate— or I thought so at the time....

"So I'm going to hear about every mouthful you ate and drank," Ern complained. "How about the pup? What did he have for supper?"

"Johnny gave him a hunk of bread," I said, like I didn't understand her. "Then he took off on business of his own."

"Oh, get on with it!" she laughed. "You know what I want to hear!"

Well, Johnny laid back with his head on his pack and shut his eyes. He looked comfortable and I was looking forward to doing the same after I unrolled the sleeping bag I brought from the barge. Knew if I stretched out without it, I'd spend the night without it and be pretty sore in the morning.

"I could sleep on the ground just as I am," Johnny says.

"Better not," I'm saying— just normal stuff like that— "better not," when Buster bounces in among us again and starts licking Johnny's face like he hadn't seen him for a week.

"Here! Get off!" Johnny howls, and pushes the mutt away.

Well, I'm unlacing the first boot and feeling glad the pup attached himself to Johnny and not to me. I'm thinking in a minute I'm going to lie down in a nice, warm sleeping bag. I'm looking forward to it. I'm going to stretch every muscle— they're all aching. I'm going to close my eyes, think of nothing....

And this little kid's voice says, "That your dog, Mister?"

"Go away, kid," I say. "We're going to sleep now."

"Is that your dog?" he says again.

"No," Johnny says. "He's not our dog. We never saw him before in our lives."

"Oh! Then can I have him?" the kid squeals, real excited.

"Sure," Johnny tells him. "You can have him. If he wants to stay with you. If your mother says so."

"Honest?" the kid hollers. "Can I?"

"Honest," Johnny says. "Go find your mother."

He laughs and closes his eyes again, but the kid doesn't take the hint. Instead he pokes him in the shoulder with a stiff little finger. Tough little customer.

"Here!" Johnny says. "What are you doing? I said you could have him. You don't need to poke holes in me to prove it. You can have him."

"You tell him that," the kid says. "He doesn't want to come with me."

"That's because we just gave him his supper," I said. "You wait a bit and offer him a snack. Then he'll come, running."

"Honest?"

"Sure."

Well, the kid wiggled all over with excitement. "Missy!" he hollered.

Johnny laughed and stretched.

I went on taking my boots off and listened to the kid running over rough ground. Cute little fellow. But I hated to think what his mother was going to say! Figured Johnny was tempting fate and it wouldn't take long to get results.

And then, just the other side of the bushes, this cool, soft voice speaks. And I start a whole new stage of my existence!

"There, Missy!" the little fellow is shouting. "By the rocks. Right there. And the man said I could have him. Honest he did. So he's mine now, isn't he."

"But what would we do with a dog on the boat, Cally?" this cool voice says. "I don't think the barge men would let us take him on the boat."

"He could look after us," the kid argues. "And bite the bad men."

I pulled my boots back on and stood up.

By then the kid's poking Johnny's shoulder again and Johnny's struggling to his feet. But I'm only seeing them out of the corner of my eye. What I'm looking at is this girl— like I never saw another girl in all my life....

"Stop right there," Ern says. "What's she like?"

I think I coloured up.

"Well, young," I said. "Fair like the boy. Brown from the sun."

"Aw, come on," Ern scoffed. "You can do better than that!"

I thought a minute.

"Ern," I said then, "if you really want to know, she's something..."

"Of course she is," Ern says, with this big grin. "The question is, what is she?"

"Well," I said, "her hair is the colour of moth wings. Was I telling you about the moths Jenny was dancing with up to Wooji? Well, that colour. And she had it braided over her shoulder in this thick plait. And she looked at me out of these deep blue, sober eyes, that I didn't have to look away down to see."

"She sounds just right," Ern said.

"I didn't think I'd ever meet her, Ern," I said, "and I guess I just stood with my mouth open.   If I did, she probably didn't notice because she was naturally looking at the kid and Johnny..."

"Did you give Cally your puppy?" Missy says.

"Not exactly," Johnny tells her, "but if you'll allow him to have the mutt, he's welcome. The boy seems to have taken a shine to him."

"And cats. And snails. And bugs and worms," she says, but she's smiling. "And anything else that moves."

Then she looked at me too, kind of worried. "Why are you sitting in the dark?" she says.

"We just got here before the sun went down," Johnny told her, "and we haven't had time or energy to light a fire, though we bought some wood."

"You've just come?" she cries, sort of panicky. "But you're barge men, aren't you? Your boots... Is there a barge in?"

"No," I said. "There isn't a barge and won't be till the rains come. The water's low and the nearest barge is stranded three days down the water."

Her shoulders drooped. "I didn't really think so," she said. "Always the whole camp knows when a barge comes in."

"Did it mean so much to you?" Johnny asks.

"No," she says, kind of hopeless. "It was just a wild idea."

"We need a fire," Johnny says. "That will cheer us up." And he reaches for our makings.

"That little bundle won't last very long," Missy says. "But if you want to add it to mine... You'd better bring all your things along to my camp. Otherwise the guards will give you a hard time for sleeping without a tent."

I had no doubt of that.

"It's friendlier too," she said. "And safer, I think."

She was giving me the horrors.

"How long have you been here?" Johnny asks her.

"Oh, not very long really," she says. "Two months or so. But it's been nice summer weather. And I almost got passage a few days ago. There was a barge going down and the owner said she'd take us. But she changed her mind at the last minute and took a single man instead. Tillie Vetchcum, her name was."

I shuddered.

"The passie had a sack of something," she said. "Acrite pods, I imagine— anyway he acted shifty. It was a big sack. He'll make a fortune in the City."

She walked on ahead with Johnny, carrying one of our bags, and Cally followed with the pup, the grub bag, and me. He chattered, but I didn't hear much of what he said. My mind was in a turmoil— not to speak of all the rest of me!!

Pretty soon we came to a tent in a small depression behind a rock wall that shut out the light. It was already dark in there.

"Wait till I light the fire," Missy says, and she goes ahead a few steps into the hollow.

It was very quiet. You could hear voices right across the valley and a howl a long way off. I could have howled myself.

"Make yourselves at home," she says, when the flames burned up.

"It's very good of you to share your fire," Johnny says.

"To tell the truth, I'm lonely," she told him, "and just a little scared. I'm glad you've come..."

"Oh, Arnold," Ern whispers.

"It fair made the hair on the back of my neck stand up, Ern," I said.

"What was she thinking of! Making friends with strangers. Inviting two guys she never saw in her life before to share her fire."

"I wanted to start right in and give her a good lecture," I said. "But that was before I knew... Well, before I knew a lot about Missy that I found out later. Not that I ever got over thinking that way though!"

For a minute I was back there with her. "I should never have let her out of my sight, Ern," I said.

"No, well, that's you, Arnold."

"Was, Ern. Was," I said, and I think she believed me after all...

We sat by the campfire.

Johnny and Missy talked. I guess I was still tongue-tied.

After awhile Cally lays his head on Missy's lap and yawns. "Story," he mutters, pointing at Johnny. "Story."

"A bedtime story?" Johnny says, looking like what you might call nonplussed.

"Yes... Please."

Johnny laughed. "Are you going to stay awake long enough to listen?" he says.

"Yes... Promise."

"Well, then... Once upon a time..."

"Yes."

"Once upon a time there was a little boy called Johnny."

"That was you," the kid says. He's fighting to keep his eyes open.

"Johnny had black curls... And blue eyes... And a very beautiful mother. And Johnny and his mother came down from the Maglev Hills and camped in a valley."

The kid nodded.

"Johnny was very happy in the valley. All day he ran and played. And in the evening his mother made a fire, and cooked his supper, and put his sweater on him."

"Uh-huh."

"Johnny was only five then, and small, and his mother took great care of him. But he loved all sorts of bugs, and birds, and animals, and he never felt afraid."

"Just like me," the kid mutters.

"And one night an old man came to the campfire and sat down beside Johnny and his mother."

Even Missy was listening by this time.

"This old man," Johnny says, "was a very old man. Dark and shadowy. But he was kind and good. And he had a beautiful big cat with him. A monstrous cat. Johnny thought it must be the biggest cat in the whole world."

The little fellow's eyes opened at that!

"When he stood up close to it, and the cat was sitting down," Johnny said, "Johnny's eyes looked straight into the cat's eyes. And the cat's eyes were golden. And shiny. His fur was golden too. But his ears were black. And he had black lines around his eyes. Black... lines... around... his eyes... and his whiskers shone... all shimmery... in the firelight."

For a minute it looked like the story-teller was going to be asleep first, but he went on with the story.

"Johnny, and the cat, and the old man," he said, "all loved each other very much. And the cat purred and said 'Hello, Johnny. How are you? I'm your friend."

"And Johnny said, 'Hello, cat. I like you very much. Do you mind if I touch your nose, sir?' And the cat said, 'It would be a pleasure, little friend. Please do."

Cally smiled and fell asleep, and Johnny sat staring into the fire.

After a long while he said, "My mother was afraid."

"Of course she was!" Missy exclaimed. "I don't blame her. I would be too."

Johnny looked at her, surprised.

Then she laughed. "I'm sorry," she said. "It's just that I don't believe in telling lies to children... That was... only a story... Wasn't it?"

Chapter: 3

Next morning early Mrs. Presking's hens were clucking and scratching in the dirt behind her house. A ginger cat perched on a fence post, blinking at the sun. And three pink hollyhocks bloomed by the kitchen door.

I felt happy. Probably looked it.

Mrs. Presking didn't look happy though. She was standing in her back door in a dark dress, with a basket of white eggs in her hand. Her eyes were narrowed. Maybe against the low sun, but I don't think so. More likely against the two of us approaching with packs on our backs and Missy, Cally, and the pup in tow. Anyway she had a look of "here's-trouble-coming" on her face.

"Morning, Mrs. Presking."

"I never seen you lot before," she said. "Nor you're not bargees, neither, except maybe for the big one there. For I think I know a bargeman when I see one. What you wanting here?"

"To begin with, Mrs. Presking," Johnny said, "breakfast. Then rooms for our stay in Canalhead. Some of us may be here for quite awhile."

"Indeed, now," she says. "And will you dictate to a poor widow woman on her very doorstep?"

"Not at all, Ma'am," Johnny says, smiling. "I propose a strictly business arrangement."

"Ten credits a day. Each!" she snapped. "Five for the child. No animals in the house. And dog scraps extra."

I had all I could do not to holler "Highway robbery!" and Missy gasped, but Johnny was in charge.

"That's a high price, Mrs. Presking," he said, "but I'll agree to it. Let's start with breakfast."

"Not so fast, young man," Mrs. Presking says. "Not before I see the first month's credits in my hand. Pay now, eat later."

"The credits will be next door at the Business Bank," Johnny says. "You may draw half in advance and half at the end of each week for as long as we stay."

At that Mrs. Presking drew a deep breath. But Cally and the pup had their noses to the wire netting around the chicken coop, and the dog barked.

She swooped on them like a big black crow!

Then, with the hens rescued, she turned on the rest of us. "We'll see the banker when he comes down," she said. "In the meantime, you can sit on the bank verandah. There's chairs there for customers— and loafers."

"The meantime will be just about right for us to have our breakfast," Johnny says. "We're not hard to please. Those eggs would be good."

I turned away so Mrs. Presking wouldn't see me smile and wasn't prepared when she shied away from Johnny and started in on Missy instead.

"Don't know about you, girl," she snapped. "Never take females. Nor never had a child before, neither. Not in thirty years."

But Cally turned from the hens and gazed at her, and gradually her face sort of smoothed out, almost like it was trying to remember smiling.

"Well," she muttered, "never mind. The rain's coming, ain't it. And he's just a wee mite. No more than a baby hardly."

"I'm five years old!" Cally told her.

At that, Mrs. Presking chuckled. Took a second to do it, but she chuckled, and the smile was close.

She chuckled, but she made it up by turning on Missy again. "You'll have to keep him out of my kitchen," she warned. "That understood? And no dogs past the doorstep."

Missy smiled. She looked very like Cally when she smiled and something tightened in my chest. "Thank you, Mrs. Presking," she said. "Thank you very much."

"Humph," Mrs. Presking grunted, but she moved out of the way and let us in.

Well, that morning was like a spring day off. We ate, showered, changed. Visited the bank, the shops, and the shipping office. Got looked over by everybody in the square, and had one hell of a good time.

Even met the manager of The Marshlands in the hardware store.

"Good morning, gentlemen," he says, all smiles—didn't recognize us clean! "Enjoying our stay in Canalhead, are we?"

"Been thrown out of the best places in town," I told him, and got a big kick out of doing it.

Everywhere we went Buster followed. If we disappeared into a building out of reach, he galloped back to the house and hid behind a cucumber vine at the end of the front verandah. Back and forth, back and forth. By noon he was played out. Couldn't drag his tail behind him! Which Cally made up for with demonstrations of affection that played him out still more.

But that afternoon black vapour appeared over the hills and gusts of cold wind stirred the dust in the square.

Cally and I were eating ice cream up by the hotel when the first one swept down upon us. I wondered about it. But then the weather seemed to clear and Cally and I continued with our shopping.

We were in the clothing store when the first rumble of thunder rolled over the town.

"Soldiers!" Cally whispered.

I didn't pay much attention. "No," I said. "Thunder. In the sky. You know."

He shivered.

"Cold?" I asked.

But he didn't answer. He was listening.

The wind picked up and more thunder echoed in the hills.

"Guess we'd better get home before the rain starts," I said. "Ready, mate?"

I took his hand, and it was cold as ice.

"There are no soldiers, Cally," I told him. "Not here. OK?"

I thought he believed me, but back at the house we found nobody home and he almost had a fit.

"Missy's all right," I told him. "She'll be back soon. Let's see if Mrs. Presking made some cookies."

"No," he whispered. "Soldiers. Hide."

He ran out into the yard calling Missy, and a gust of wind pinned him against the hen-run fence. I picked him off the wire crying and struggling for breath.

"You and me are mates now, Cally," I said. "I'll help you look after Missy. Won't be any soldiers to worry about when I'm around. Let's see if we can find the cookies."

"No."

Just then a louder rumble sounded, and he dove into the house and hid behind the kitchen door.

"Never mind," I said. "It really isn't soldiers. But you can hide there if you want to."

I had things to do around the house. Kept an eye out for the little fellow though, and every now and then I'd catch a glimpse of him peeking out at me around the door.

Slowly the light failed. Lightening flashed. Thunder rolled nearer. Gusts of wind whipped around the house. One wrenched off the front gate. Another took the cucumber trellis. One by one the hollyhocks disappeared.

After awhile Mrs. Presking came home with a load of shopping, all out of breath.

"We'll eat early," she gasped, "and let the fire out, for it'll blow this evening something terrible... Isn't that girl back yet?!"

She looked worried.

"What do you mean?" I demanded. "Where is she?"

"My Lord, get after her!" she panted. "She started out for the campground."

Missy!

I hared out through the dump and up the ridge.

Up there the strange light coming through the rags of the storm made every needle on the old pine stand out singly, every flake of bark separate. It was like the day the duster flattened Wooji, and I nearly had heart failure.

But Missy was struggling up the other side of the ridge.

Her hair was blown out of the braid and wound around her head like a halo, and I figured I was seeing what she really was— angels seeming to keep turning up in the most unlikely places.

I wrestled her pack off her back and onto mine, and got an arm around her so she could shelter her face in my shoulder and get her breath. But we kept on moving as fast as we could through it all.

Nearer the house I could see Mrs. Presking holding the back door open and calling to us. Couldn't hear what she was saying, but the downpour was coming and I guessed it was that. Cally was hanging onto her skirt and peeking out around her. Poor little Buster was crying on the doorstep.

We dove through the doorway just as the first rain and hail struck. Couldn't hardly hear the door slam for the racket, let alone what anybody said, but it was clear enough what Cally wanted.

"Buster?" he whimpered, looking up at Mrs. P with big tears in his eyes.

She hesitated, but only for a moment.

"Oh, all right, then," she muttered. "I suppose he'll have to come in."

She scowled, but Cally reached up and gave her a hug. And I'm sure— dead sure by the face of her— that that hug was her first since Presking-bargee went to his final rest— if not a long while before that. I figured she was thawing out kindly!

Cally didn't notice, of course— too busy finding a place for Buster to hide behind a pair of old marsh boots. Then he ran to Missy.

"Soldiers," I heard him whisper.

"No, Cally," she said. "No soldiers here. Only the sky noise. Don't be afraid."

She was trembling herself, though, and she sat down in a big chair and drew Cally onto her knees. I wanted to put my arms around them both and hold them, but the best I could do was to wrap one of Mrs. Presking's crocheted what-u-ma-callums around them. Expected to catch a tongue lashing for spoiling the arrangements, but nothing was said.

Johnny showed up while I was wrapping them and grinned at me but didn't say a word, which was a good thing— for him.

Slowly the light failed altogether. Thunder crashed. Gusts of wind shook the house. A shutter from the general store rolled end over end past the front window, and a garden swing from behind the bank landed against a corner of the verandah with an almighty thump.

Then the rain came in earnest. It poured off the roof and ran in brown streams down the square. It seemed almost solid. I was afraid Cally would be scared to death, but when the rain started he calmed down. Even left Missy's knee and came and looked out the window with me.

"Soldiers don't like raining," he said, and smiled up at me.

I took his hand and it was warm again.

It was quite a show out there in the square, but pretty soon Mrs. Presking called us to supper, which we ate at the kitchen table by the light of an oil lamp.

Johnny started questioning Mrs. P and Missy about the weather. How long would the rains last? How long would the winter last? How long before winter came?

I let my mind wander.

After awhile Cally got down and spent a few minutes comforting Buster. When he came back he had a piece of brown paper in one hand— a bag that some of our shopping came home in— and a stump of crayon in the other. And as we sat around the table talking, he drew our pictures. I remember he did a pretty good job of Johnny— at least, you could tell who he was by the masses of curls on his head.

Then he began to make letters. And pretty soon he pushed the paper toward me and said, "That's my name."

Sure enough, he had written C-A-L-L-Y.

"Smart kid," I said.

"Now I'll do my father's name," he told me.

I was not interested in Cally's father. As far as I was concerned, Cally had no business having a father. In my opinion, the world could do without the fellow altogether. But in a few minutes back came the paper with B-R-U-N-O written on it.

"That's my father's name, isn't it, Missy?" he said.

Missy glanced at the paper and nodded.

"Now I'll do my mother," Cally told me. "You can watch me if you want to."

So I watched. What else could I do?

First came L. Then O. Then U-I-S-A.

"Louisa," Cally said. "Did I do it right?"

"That your real name?" I said to Missy. "Louisa?"

"No, no," she said. "No. My name is Melissa."

I jumped like I put my finger in a light socket. My face probably lit up like it too. Anyway, Missy's cheeks turned pink and Johnny grinned ear to ear, while Mrs. Presking's sharp eyes travelled around the table several times and jumped to about a hundred and fifty-one conclusions.

Missy's cheeks stayed pink, but she smiled at me. "Louisa was my sister," she said.

A gust of wind shook the house to its foundations and thunder rolled in one side of my head and out the other, but I would have sworn I never saw a nicer night.

Well, Cally carried on drawing, and the others kept on talking, but I took no further interest. I suppose I never took my eyes off Missy. Anyway, I don't remember much till the party broke up.

Johnny went upstairs first and slept like a baby in spite of the earth-shaking events that were taking place around him.

Then Missy took Cally up to bed. She was gone quite a long time, long enough for Mrs. Presking and me to wash the supper dishes.

"That's a nice girl," Mrs. P told me, as she handed me the dishtowel. "And don't you forget it."

I felt hurt, insulted. And I was just opening my mouth to start in defending the purity of my intentions, when she took off on another subject altogether.

"Been expecting Jody Ruddin," she said. "Why don't he come himself?"

"Jody's dead, Mrs. Presking," I muttered.

"Dead. Ah, is it so? That was a good man, Jody," she told me. "And a good master too, as I know for a fact. Nature, or the canal, boy?"

"Canal," I said. "Bay sixteen, on the passing cable."

"I thought so," she said, and looked out the window at the storm but not seeing it. "So 'twas Jody. I knew of trouble on the water. The singing broke my rest."

Her sharp eyes misted over, but not before she saw the expression on my face.

"Don't go very deep with you, does it," she said. "You're not a bargee, though you've the markings. What was it? Bad luck as a child? Orphans sometimes..."

"No," I said. "My sister and I were orphans pretty young, but we didn't come from a barge family. Lived around the canals, that's all. Picked up a little of the..."

"Wisdom," she finished for me. "Wisdom."

"If you like," I said.

"Don't matter what anybody likes," she snapped. "'Tis so."

She wiped her eyes on her apron. "You'd better tell me how it was," she said.

It wasn't something I wanted to remember...

About noon.

Sixth day out from the den.

We were playing cards with some of the crew, when Jody lays down his hand and stands up listening.

The others watch him, trying to read his thoughts.

He walks off to starboard, puts his right ear to the deck, and listens. After a few minutes he walks to the other side and lays his left ear to the deck.

"He hears something," one of them whispered to us.

After that he climbed to the galley roof and looked ahead. Stayed there five, six minutes, not moving. Then he raised one hand above his head with the fingers spread and the thumb forward. Meet. About ten lengths up the water. I knew the sign.

We watched him come down and stand on the deck like he was mapping out the future in his mind.

"Can we help?" Johnny says.

"Naw," Jody says, with a big grin. "This is man's work." But he gives Johnny a friendly clout on the back.

Then he changes his mind. "On second thoughts," he says, "that might be a good idea. If you two was to come forward with me, I could put the young fellow with old Laddy, and Pad could lend a hand at the port-forward winch— she's a bitch when the water's low."

We didn't wait for anything more but followed him down a narrow passage between piles of crates and bales to the prow peak. Up there the clanking of cables was very loud.

"What's going on?" Johnny hollers.

Jody laughs. "Haven't you heard her groan these two or three hours?" he says.

"No," Johnny says. "Was there a difference?"

"Difference between night and day!" Jody hoots. "This here's a mech section, see? There's free sections and there's mech sections. The closer we come to the head, the more mech sections we come on. They lift us from height to height. Closer we come to Canalhead, more we have to climb against the stream. What we're doing now, you see, we're taking branch cable to lay over for Tillie Vetchcum coming by. Wait till you see Tillie go. She'll be bowling along like a cork in a bathjet.

"Stoned to the eyeballs, like as not," he added, as if to himself. "We'll take no chance with Tillie."

All the time he was talking he was watching the water just below the prow.

"Here, you two," he says, after a few minutes. "Lay down here and tell me what you see. Steady now."

Well, five or six feet down, the surface of the water was bubbling with marsh gas rising to the surface.

"Talk," Jody orders. "Tell me what you see."

"Brown water," Johnny says. "Bubbles. Bits of plants."

"Go on," Jody says. "Keep talking. I see it too, but I'm looking forward of you. Look right down below the prow."

"Water," Johnny says. "Brown water. Bubbles."

"Good."

"Blue spots!" I yell.

"God! You sure?"

"They're gone now," I say. "But I'm sure. Bright blue spots about as big as a silver dollar."

Jody groans and shouts down the barge. "Mudshells!"

I'd heard of them, of course. Anybody's ever been around barges has heard of mudshells. And it didn't sound good.

The rest of the crew agreed with me, and three or four of them left their stations and ran forward.

"The passing cable is only about a barge length ahead," Jody says. "We'll have time enough if Tillie's not sliding full speed on. But I think she is. I think she is!"

They all shook their heads.

"We should have time," Jody says again, "but that's Tillie, sure as water's wet, and I feel it in my bones, there's trouble coming. Every man in insulboots and mitts, helmets on and fastened. And all hands lashed on a short line."

They all flew down the deck and Jody watched them out of sight among the lots of cargo.

"They won't like it," he muttered, "but they'll do it. And not just because I say so. They know. Any bargee worth his salt is scared witless of them blue dancers when they get fouled of the power lines. 'Mudshells. Trouble. And lily eels."

I'd heard that saying on the canals, but those blue spots rising in the water ahead of our prow were my first direct experience of mudshells— and I didn't like them, even on that much acquaintance.

"See them webbing harnesses there?" Jody says. "They're fastened to the deck. Slip into them now the way you see me do. We don't want you flying off the bows."

So we lay in the harnesses as the barge moved slowly forward and the oily blue spots rose to the surface of the water.

"What are they?" Johnny shouted.

"Mudshells," Jody grumbled. "Multiply when the water's low and foul the lines. Sometimes get so thick they clog the cable. Electric scourers on the bottom kills them as we go— long's they're not too thick. Just... so they're not... too... thick."

The barge inched forward.

Jody watched the sky and the grass ahead.

Twice he put his ear to the deck.

"She's coming on too fast," he muttered the second time.

At that moment, the barge shuddered, and stopped.

"Fouled!" he roared.

He threw off his harness and started back.

Johnny and I turned our heads to watch him go. That's why we didn't see Tillie's prow coming down on us till she started by.

She struck us amidships.

Mudshells blew out of the water!

Lily eels as thick as my arm sailed into the air! One of them was in two pieces, and stinking purple blood spurted over us.

The noise was terrible! It seemed like the whole world was screaming.

Then silence.

The eels still thrashed in the water. The mudshells plopped on the surface. The marsh grass swayed. But all in total silence.

I looked around.

Our barge was lying stern-in to the port bank, across the stream. She smelled of burnt-out power cable, but there didn't seem to be fire aboard and we weren't going to sink.

Tillie Vetchcum's barge, though, was on her side, rammed into the opposite bank. You wouldn't believe it, knowing how big those barges are.

Johnny was beside me, battered but living.

"You Ok?" I yelled.

"What?" he says. "I can't hear you."

"What?" I say. "I can't hear you!"

Then a column of smoke started out of Tillie's cargo hold, and almost at the same time flames leapt into the grass.

"Man the sluices," I yelled.

I felt the words in my throat, but I couldn't hear them.

Johnny grabbed me so I'd look at him and know what he was saying.

"Cover your face," he yelled. "Wet yourself all over. Wet the barge. Are the pumps working?"

We found three of the crew alive and drove them to work the pumps by hand. We tied wet rags over their faces and hosed them down. Forced them to live.

They kept shaking their heads. And they were muttering to themselves. I couldn't hear, but I thought I knew what they were saying. Defeated things. But we needed them. Everybody had to fight the fire or we didn't have a chance.

The wind was with us, blowing across us toward the other side. But sparks fell on our deck and we had to stamp them out. Johnny climbed to the roof of the galley and fought a fire there. I put out flames in a pile of bales forward.

It didn't take long, but it seemed like the rest of my life at the time. And when it was over and the flames were eating their way across the marsh away from us, we started in to shake. It was a terrible feeling. Shock, I suppose.

My throat burned. The pain in my ears was so bad I howled but still I couldn't hear myself. Bits of singed hair fell in my eyes and mouth if I moved. And I felt dead tired— about a hundred years old.

Johnny had a deep cut on his left arm above the elbow.

But the shaking was the worst. We huddled against the galley wall and shook, and couldn't stop.

When the sun went down, the night was cold. But still we sat there shaking.

Some time before morning, when we were starting to hear again, there was singing— sort of chanting— then splashing and thrashing in the water. I figured I knew what it was. Didn't tell Johnny, but I think he knew. Anyway, he never asked me later what happened to Jody.

By daylight our barge was drifted a little farther into the bank. What was left of Tillie's was sunk deeper in the mud— there was just its ribs and keel. And the marsh was black for miles..

"Abandon ship, I guess?" Johnny says.

Didn't see what else we could do.

We looked for what was left of the crew, but they were all out of it. I hauled one to his feet but had to drop him back. Acrite, I suppose...

Mrs. Presking nodded and wiped her eyes on her apron.

"Aye," she said. "So be it. He was a good man, Jody."

Neither of us had been thinking much about what we were doing, but the dishes went on being washed and polished. And by the time Missy came back Mrs. P was hanging up the towels on a rod behind the stove and I was just picking up Cally's brown paper and wondering if it was precious or if I should put it in the trash.

Besides the names and the pictures of us, there was this other drawing. I couldn't make much of it. Seemed to be a man with a rifle in his hand. A soldier, I thought. Then there was a small boy, no doubt Cally. And a woman with her hand raised with something in it— a gun, maybe, or a knife. She was looking at the soldier and he was falling down.

"I guess we'd better keep this," I said. "He'll probably want it in the morning."

Missy looked. And her face went white. No, worse than white. Gray. Almost green. I thought she was going to fall.

"Missy!" I cried, and got my arm around her. But she pulled away and ran out of the room...

"So that was Missy when I first saw her, Ern," I said, "and I didn't sleep very well that night."

Ern laughed. "I'm glad you told me," she said. "Do you think you can sleep tonight?"

Probably not, now that I've started thinking about her," I said. "It's so close. I mean, I should be seeing her inside of two weeks— if she's still there."

"You did look after her," Ern said. "Found her a place to stay or something."

"Of course," I said. "I left her with Mrs. Presking... But she doesn't know!"

Ern grinned. "Tell me," she says. "This girl is of average intelligence? Not some dumb blonde or something?"

"Of course not!" I growled.

"Then she knows," Ern says, and she musses up my hair on her way to bed. She was grinning at me the way Johnny used to do when I first... well... "Don't worry, honey," she says. "She knows. Anybody as transparent as you..."

Red Dragon Square

Part 3

"And the parched ground shall become a pool, and the thirsty land springs of water: in the habitation of dragons, where each lay, shall be grass with reeds and rushes." (Isaiah 35:7)

Chapter: 1

After Ern staggered to her room that night, I dragged myself to the sleepout, threw my shirt over Cranky, and stretched out on my bed. Didn't sleep though. Felt like I must've been drowning, the way my life kept reeling in front of my eyes.

Couldn't get over how— almost said "lucky"— I was. I mean, the second Jacon Jaconi could have come to grief a dozen times, just getting to Canalhead. We could've gone to the lily eels when the barge struck. We could've gone up in the fire. My Lord, as Mrs. Presking would say, we could've turned back!

We could have come to a nasty end the second morning, just before daybreak, when we paddled past Dobby at the last canalden. Johnny looked black enough to go aboard and start the fight all over again. But by that time we both knew what would happen if they threw us into the mechcanal, with or without a length of chain around our neck!

For awhile we expected to hear Dobby coming up behind us, but pretty soon we saw he wouldn't be coming. Not till the rains brought more water into the system— which they did. One afternoon we were down at the docks watching the sights and ran right into him. Pretended he didn't know us. Gave us a wide berth though. Johnny's still laughing about that.

We laughed a lot those weeks at Mrs. Presking's. They were good time. Buster grew. Cally started school. Missy got a job at the bakery. As for me, I never went out without my boots on for fear of lifting off the ground and floating away.

Johnny was happy enough too. Impatient to be on his way but not making misery for himself and everybody else because he couldn't. Slept well. Not wearing rose-coloured glasses— like I was— but... well... what you might call rolling with the punches. Spent his time buttonholing passies and putting the questions to them. Where did they come from? How long since they left, wherever it was. Did they ever hear of the Moonstream? Thought he was crazy, of course. Harmless. But crazy.

When he wasn't doing that, it seemed to me he went around with a foolish grin on his face. That was more than I could understand, till the day he said, "The rains are coming to an end, mate. I'll be moving out soon. You don't have to come with me, you know."

"I guess I will," I said.

"You don't have to."

"No, but I never had a reason for anything I did before..."

I was thinking about that, looking at it all around, when these palm trees started sprouting all over Canalhead, this ocean cruise ship pulled into the docks, and Missy got off wearing a white gown and orange blossoms in her hair. I was there all dolled up in a tapestry waistcoat and a string tie. My hair was curling over my collar, and I had this long, silky moustache that got tangled in Missy's orange blossoms. I was just trying to untangle myself so I could kiss her when she's Ern in jeans and a white shirt.

"Come on, come on," she's saying. "Are you going to sleep all day? Morning threw the rocks in the bowl of night hours ago, and Baldy will be here soon... Should I bring the sofa set, do you think?"

Lord love us! Sofa sets!

I tried to talk sense into her but ended up saying I'd take her out to Hawberry to see for herself.

"Good," she says. "Why don't you take Su up on her offer of the convertible. Then we can take a few things with us, sort of head start.

"Alice is my only hope," I thought.

Hope! They took to each other like twin sisters separated at birth.

"I wanted to ask you about the sofa set," Ern started in. "Arnold thinks..."

"No, dear," Alice says. "Definitely not. I know what you're going to say and it's a mistake. I left a lot of things back in Hill City when we came here, and I've been sorry ever since. You think you'll replace them but you don't."

"Then we'll have to buy a truck!" I howled.

"That's a great idea!" Ern says. "That way there'll be lots of room. Besides ours, you know, there'll be Su's own stuff, and I know for a fact she's been shopping like crazy for Jenny. Then when Missy joins us..."

"Missy?" says Alice, looking puzzled. "George told us about Johnny's Mum and Jenny, but..."

"Oh, Missy's Arnold's girl," Ern says, off-hand. "We'll be picking her up later."

"Arnold! Why didn't you tell us, dear!" Alice hollers, all smiles.

"I'm going out to buy a truck," I said. "Coming Budd?"

He came, but he was grinning ear to ear. Why is it people grin all over their faces the minute a pretty girl is mentioned!

"So you're joining the ranks!" he bellows, as soon as we're outside the door. And he gives me this thump across the shoulders that nearly drives me through the boardwalk.

I was ready to wring Ern's neck!

But when we got back, after adding a two-ton truck to the fleet of George and Co., supper was almost ready and the kids were all washed and brushed, and listening wide-eyed to their Auntie Ern holding forth. She was buttering rolls and looking like it wouldn't melt in her mouth.

"So, Budd," she says, "Alice has been telling me Arnold and Johnny stayed with you folks up to Hill City three years ago."

"Sure did," Budd says. "Enjoyed having them. Must have been with us five or six weeks."

"Ten weeks and three days," Bob said.

"That long!" Budd says, sounding surprised.

"We were up on Maundy the first time we saw them," Alice said, with a smile for me. "Needed feeding up, I thought."

"And you were making pancakes," I reminded her...

I woke up because somebody was giggling. Opened one eye, and they all ran away! Didn't move, and they came back.

"Ma sent us to fetch you to breakfast," the little girl said. "We knew where to find you 'cause Daddy said you'd be sleeping so you could keep one eye up the Hellish."

"Did you ever hear it called the Moonstream?" Johnny asked.

"No. It's the Hellish. 'Cause the water is swift and the logs get caught in the bends and stick."

"Our Uncle Janos got lost in the Hellish once," the second boy said, "and Matty Heeny's father broke his leg."

"We're the Atherton kids," the big boy told us. "I'm Jack, and this is Bob, and that's Maudy. You can tell we're all one family."

They were peas in a pod. Straight red hair, pale gray eyes, freckles, and not an ounce of fat among them.

They stood and watched as we rolled our sleeping bags.

"Come on," Bob said, "Ma's making pancakes. I can eat sixteen. How many can you eat?"

The boys ran around us, kicking up dry leaves, but Maudy walked backwards ahead of us, keeping just out of reach, and studying us closely.

"What's the matter?" Johnny asked. "Are you afraid we'll bite?"

"No," she said. "You wouldn't bite us. Not enough meat on us to make it worth your while. Ma says we're eating her out of house and home but we run it off... You got black curls."

"Morning!" Budd called from the verandah of a log cabin. Behind the cabin the valley opened up into a deep bowl, and a stream thundered out of a hanging valley still hidden in early mist. Straight pines grew to tremendous heights. This was real mountains. I'd never seen anything like it before and didn't know what to make of it. But Johnny was glowing. Watching him I felt glad I came, even with Missy curled up in the back of my mind.

"This is a beautiful place," I said.

"Isn't it?" Budd agreed. "But come and meet the missis. Drove out in the pickup with the kids to visit me. Thought I might be lonesome out here all by myself. What do you think of that?"

Alice's cheeks coloured as she came onto the verandah wiping her hands on her apron. It was easy to see where the kids got their looks, and their energy.

"Come and have some breakfast," she said. "You must be starved. And don't mind Budd. He'd like to think we couldn't do without him."

At the table, Maudy manoeuvred herself next to Johnny. "You got a mother?" she asked.

"What?" Johnny said. "Me? Oh, yes. I have a mother. Her name is Su."

"Can she make pancakes?"

I had to smile. Couldn't quite picture Su frying pancakes. Johnny seemed to find it hard to picture too.

"I don't know, Maudy," he said. "I've never seen her do it, but I guess she could if she tried. She's pretty smart."

"What does she make you for breakfast then?" she asked.

"Well," Johnny said, "we generally eat... Well, stuff from the kitchen. You know. Sometimes one thing, sometimes another. Milk... Coffee... Buns..."

"You mean your mother can't cook," Maudy said. "That's too bad. Our mother can cook real good. You hadn't ought to of married her if she can't cook."

Bob giggled, and Jack said, "Maudy! Don't you know yet that people don't marry mothers?"

"Daddy married ours," Maudy argued.

"But I wasn't your mother then," Alice told her. "A mother is a lady who looks after you when you're little. Are you talking about the lady that looked after Johnny then or the one that looks after him now?"

Maudy studied Johnny's face. Then she sighed and said she guessed his little mother must be pretty old by now so probably she meant his other one.

Everybody hooted with laughter, even Johnny. There was no pain for Jenny in his face. I wondered about that. Something happened at the pool, down below— though I wasn't clear on just what, yet.

But Maudy's ears went pink. Tears came in her eyes. And I saw Johnny slip his hand over hers under the table.

"I'll tell you about them both some time if you like," he whispered.

"Oh, yes!" she whispered back. "Please. I think you're lovely."

"Never forget the night I picked them up and hauled them home," Budd was saying. "Half way over Maundy. Figured they lost their way. I mean, up there with only backpacks and winter coming on. Took them for loggers out of a job, not a couple of babes in the woods looking for the Moonstream.

"No telling how long it took them to get that far..."

Five days from the Mirror Pool, if time exists there.

We came up out of the ravine at a place where the stream crossed a logging road. The sun was already moving down the west. Under the canopy of trees, dark was coming on.

We were more than half way over Maundy, nearer the top of the pass than anything, and I was thinking it looked like a cold night ahead, when I recognized this sound that was following us. Looked back, and there's this battered flatbed coming around a bend.

The cab was rusted out. The bed was chewed along the edges. But the tires looked good. And she throbbed pretty healthy under the hood.

One huge log was chained to the bed. Hadn't been felled long— thick beads of resin stood out on the ends, and it had that good smell of fresh-cut wood.

The driver changed down through the gears and stopped.

"Hop in," he hollered over the engine noise.

"Thanks," I hollered back. "Can you take two? My mate's just around the bend ahead."

He held out a big, hard hand. "Sure," he said. "Budd Atherton here. Glad to know you. Going far?"

"Not today," I said. "Just as far as the first shelter for the night."

He laughed and started up the truck. "Make that about midday tomorrow, travelling on foot," he said. "Looking for work? There's room for hands in the logging camps."

"May come to it before too long," I said.

"You young fellows!" he rumbled. "No responsibilities! Work till you've got some credits together, then off. South to the fleshpots and the bright lights."

"Hah!" I thought. "Wait till you meet my mate!"

"Heading the wrong direction, aren't you?" he went on. I pretended I didn't hear.

"Snow's not far off," he said, louder. "But they're always looking for strong hands to work the flumes."

"Thanks," I said. "We'll think about it."

"Grub's good. Pay's not bad. And the camp down the road here is well run. Warm and clean. Not much to do, of course, stuck away in the notch when the road closes. But better than nothing."

"This road is closed in winter?"

"Soon as the snow comes. Why do you think I'm dragging this great widow-maker on behind? Pay's well, that's why. I'm a married man. This'll be my last trip for the season though."

I glanced through the window in the rear of the cab and there's the log only inches away and straining and pulling at the chains.

"She won't slip," Budd says, with a big grin. "But if she does... Well, if you hear me yell, you jump. And don't look back!"

He winked and touched a good luck charm that dangled on the dash.

It was slow going. We hardly gained on Johnny for the first few minutes, and riding ahead of that log was almost as hard as walking, but it was a different pull on a different set of muscles, and on the whole I preferred the ride.

I got down when Budd stopped for Johnny, and we put him in the middle. Being a few inches taller, I needed the extra leg room. Turned out to be a convenient arrangement.

"This here's Maundy," Budd hollered over the noise of the engine.

"Maundy?"

"The mountain."

He took one hand off the wheel to indicate the spur of the mountain we were riding.

"She's called Maundy," he said. "Over there..." He ducked his head and pointed out the window past my shoulder. "Over there's Heliope. Maundy and Heliope. Hill sisters, so the story goes, and sharp of tongue and temper. So the river came between them and cut the Hellish Gap."

"The Hellish?" Johnny says sharply.

"You've heard of it?"

"I'm looking for the Moonstream," he says.

Budd glanced at him with interest. "Well, well, now," he says. "The Moonstream, is it. Figured you for a hillman. Not your friend there, but you for sure— I'm foothills bred myself. But I never took you for one of the Moonstream folks. Now that's a hill of a different contour, as the saying goes."

"Is it?" Johnny says. "I can't follow you there."

"Can't follow me," Budd says slowly. "Then you've got a lot to learn, young sir. A lot. For I know nothing at all."

"No doubt I have a lot to learn," Johnny mutters. "But what have I got to learn? That's the question."

"Don't know as I'm the one to teach you either," Budd says. "I'm just a trucker on Maundy with a wife and kids in town. What would I know about Moonstreams? But there she is if you want to see her."

He stopped the truck as we came out of a shallow cutting in the hillside and the world opened out below us. I'll remember that sight for as long as I live!

Maundy's shadow fell into the valley, and all the western side was dark, blue. But most of the east, and the heights above, glowed from the setting sun. A full moon, still white, hung over Heliope's shoulder. And far below in the valley the river ran, pure as a silver band, around the northern flank of the mountain.

Without a word we left the truck and climbed the side of the cutting to stand where the slope fell away beneath our feet.

For a long time only the snapping of the cooling engine broke the silence.

"The Moonstream!" Johnny whispered at last.

"That's her," Budd said. "Hellish Gap to the fellows trucks the logs on Maundy. Terrible place to come to grief in. But to you it's the Moonstream."

"The fair and farther Moonstream," Johnny murmured. "Where the soul of man is fashioned in the quiet heart of God."

"Yeah?" Budd says. "That what you mountain folks believe? Me, I'm just a poor boy from the foothills, where we tell our kids we found them in a cabbage patch."

Johnny laughed. "Well," he said, "I guess nobody believes the old stories any more, but that's the way it goes. God came down to see how the world was doing and found the people all huddled together at the base of the mountain trying to get up, so He took pity on them and spat out the river, and the river washed away the barrier.

"And then He put the moon high and round over the Gap to light the way, and all the people trekked on through.

"And when they reached the upper levels, they felt changed and strengthened, so they said that God had fashioned their souls in the Gap. It became a holy place, and they made songs about it."

"Don't see many trekking up the Hellish these days," Budd said, and put a hand on Johnny's shoulder. "Fact is, you're the first I ever came across."

For a few more minutes we stood looking into the Gap.

Then Budd shook his head. "Nothing but rock and wind to me," he said, "and winter coming early and staying late."

"It's the way home," Johnny answered.

"If you say so... We'll go on down now."

We didn't talk any more. Johnny and I watched the valley unfold, and Budd kept one eye on the road and one on the log, till we came to a narrow bridge where a white-water stream went leaping far down the hillside to the river.

"We'll leave her here till morning," Budd said. "Too dark now. If you want food, you'll be welcome at the camp just up the stream here. Nice friendly folks. Always stay here myself..."

"Thanks," Johnny said. "Thanks for everything. Arnold can do as he likes, of course, but I'll stay out here. You'll understand."

"Don't know as I will," Budd said, "but feel free... It's pretty in the Gap though, now I come to look at it."

Even the eastern heights were dark by this time. The sky was a sort of milky gray. And just as the legend said, the moon hung over the river to light the travellers' way.

"The Moonstream," Johnny said. "The fair and farther Moonstream..."

Maudy cuddled on my lap. "I'm glad you came back, Arnold," she whispered. "I cried when you went away."

I hugged her and she put her arms around my neck and touched the chain under my shirt.

"Oh!" she said. "Are you a prince now too?"

Before I could answer she pulled, and the medallion shone in her hand.

Her eyes opened wide. "It's the same as Johnny's!" she gasped.

"It is Johnny's."

"But doesn't he want it?"

"He doesn't need it any more."

We were talking softly, but, of course, just when you think a roomful of people are all yakking away and won't hear you, that's when there's a lull and everybody's listening.

"Mamma!" Maudy cried. "Arnold has Johnny's necklace. He says Johnny doesn't need it any more. So he's a prince now too. Why, Arnold?"

Even Ern was tongue-tied.

"Why, Arnold?"

Well, my mouth was open, but I had no idea what I was going to say, when George appeared at the door.

"Thought you might like to know there's a troupe of fire walkers came into town," he told us. "They're putting on a show in the field along the way there."

Fire walkers!

Maudy climbed onto Johnny's knee. "I promised Teacher you'd come to school tomorrow," she said.

"You what!?"

"Well, Ella Willistook is bringing the fire walkers, so I said I'd bring you."

"Oh, that's good," Bobby said. "I heard we were having a fire walk, but I didn't know we could bring company."

"Johnny's coming with me," Maudy said.

"So?" Bobby says. "Arnold can come with us. Everybody knows you're our little sister anyway."

"But much as I'd like to see the fire walkers," Johnny says, "we're no attraction. We can't sing, or do tricks, or anything like that."

"You could wear your crown," Maudy says. "You're a prince, aren't you?"

"What gives you that idea?" he says. "You know I haven't got a crown."

"You must. Teacher said you did," Maudy argued. "I told her all about you, and she said if you had three points on your star that meant you were a prince and everybody should bow when you came in."

Johnny squeezed her in a big bear hug. "If I see any bowing, you'll be for it, Maudy Atherton," he told her. "I'll have to bow back. Then you'll have to bow back. Then I'll have to bow back again... Then you'll have to..."

But Maudy was bouncing up and down on my lap.

"Oh! Can we go, Mamma?" she was begging. "Auntie Ern never saw the fire walkers, did you, Auntie Ern? You'd like them. Can we? Can we?"

"Won't be much like the day we went to school," I thought, and it wasn't. These fire walkers strolled out of a tin shed behind the Old Mill Tavern, wearing faded jeans and looking grubby. One of them needed a shave.

But I'm strolling into the courtyard of that school up to Hill City where the kids used to go. Following Johnny. Playing companion to royalty again.

He nods to a bunch of kids we know— kids who played with Bobby mostly.

They grinned and bowed, and kept their eyes on the prince.

He winked, and they giggled.

Some others bowed. Johnny bowed to them. Had to. What else could he do?

Then the whole bunch of them started in. And I'm nearly killing myself trying not to laugh, when this little girl with brown curls and big blue eyes popping, points at Johnny's bare head and squeaks, "He lost it!"

That does it! There's a gasp all around the courtyard. I can't hold back the laugh that's exploding out of me. And the bowing gets out of control altogether— till Maudy darts into the open space around the fire pit and starts in yelling, "He didn't bring it! His crown. He didn't bring it with him. His mother's keeping it. So you only have to do it once."

It took a little time.

"You only have to do it once, you know," she hollered. "Stop bowing, everybody. All you kids, stop bowing. He says you only do it once."

She flew at the rows of children. "Stop!" she shouted. "Stop! You only do it once."

Maudy was not quite six then, and little for her age, but in my estimation she grew about ten feet that day. All by herself she made the bowing stop.

And the fire master took advantage of the lull to start the show...

Out in the field behind Hawberry, the winter stars are coming out.

"Ern!" I whisper, and point upward.

Her eyes are shining. "I know," she whispers back. "George has been showing me."

It's not taking her long!

But the show is starting. The walkers poke a toe or two at the hot rocks and somebody turns on a loud speaker with a western tune whining out of it.

The walkers drop their jeans, pull off their shirts, and jump around a bit in neon-green tights that look like the odd flame has been at them. Make some magic signs with their hands— dedicating themselves to the goddess, I suppose. Then they sort of hop onto the rocks and start prancing around..

Funny how, when you've seen a really good show, it spoils you for anything else?

"They haven't any veils," Maudy whispered...

The firefly that day at school had veils, fire-coloured veils that could have been made out of flames, they were that beautiful.

She appeared from a golden coccoon, already dancing to some wild, exotic piping. Like flames herself. Her veils floated around her. Swirled, one by one. Fluttered to the ground. When she was finished prostrating herself to the goddess, they were all gone, and she leapt up in a few wisps of gauzy cloth and some strings of small brass bells.

The bells took up the rhythm of the walking and the music faded out— but not the shivers that were running up and down my spine.

The firefly was trapped on the burning rocks. Couldn't find a way of escape. Struggled to free herself. Almost succeeded. But two cruel slaves ran onto the rocks to block the way out that she found.

Slowly the firefly circled, searching. Flung herself at the invisible walls that held her. Again and again. But each time the slaves threw her back.

She weakened. Sank to the rocks. Died. And the slaves lifted her and carried her away.

In the silence afterward, all the children wiped away tears before their friends could see them crying.

Then they began to move. They ran toward the fire pit to try the air, to make sure the stones were really hot. And they darted away again. One or two boys leapt onto the rocks. Didn't stay past the first smell of burning shoe leather though. And the noise would have raised the firefly from the dead!

Maudy reached for Johnny's hand...

It was Ern, pulling me to my feet.

"Why didn't you tell me he had perfect teeth?" she whispered.

"Who?"

"George, of course," she hissed, and hurried away to walk with him—accidentally, of course..

I ended up walking home with Alice.

Passing the Hawberry Bar and Grill, where light and noise spilled out onto the street, she tried to wipe her hands on the apron that wasn't there any more. Glanced at me and smiled.

That other evening, the one after we went to school with Maudy and the boys, we found the fire walkers in the bar where Alice worked up to Hill City. Hardly knew them slumped around a table looking glum.

I was surprised. I mean, if I'd been dancing on a pile of hot rocks, I'd be running around town making sure everybody knew about it!

We stopped to talk to them and Johnny ordered drinks. One of the boys brightened up at that, but the other one still slumped, and the girl scowled.

"We saw your performance today," Johnny said.

"We know who you are," the girl muttered.

"You were very good."

"Darcie's good," the one they called Yen said. "She's the whole show. Eson and me, we're just props. But we don't mind. The old man looks after us and the work is easy."

"Easy!" I howled. "I'd hate to try it!"

"Course you would," Darcie snapped, and gave me a sour look. "Walkers are brought up to it. You're not."

"You were brought up to it?"

"Course. So was Yen and Eson. I started soon's I could stand on my feet. My Maw's a walker."

"One of the best," Yen said, and sighed.

"When she was here we got good bookings and lots of money," Darcie said. "And we never came to dumps like this."

"How do you work?" Johnny asked. "Travel in summer and stay in town in winter?"

"Yeah."

"Sounds like a good life to me," I said.

"If we went any place decent in the summer, would be," Darcie said. "But Paw won't take us south. Only into them godforsaken hills. Afraid we'll lose the power. As if we would! I bet Maw never did."

"Sure would like to get to Delta City," Yen said. "That's where Darcie's maw went. She's down there now, living it up, and we're stuck in this stinking hole. I keep telling Uncle Woofti..."

I never heard of walkers in the City.

"With spring not far off," Johnny says, "I guess you're getting ready to go back to the mountains."

Darcie curled her lip. "Mountains! I notice you had sense enough to get away. If I was a prince, you wouldn't catch me in them crawling mountains neither. It'd be downhill all the way for little Darcie."

"I'm Jaconi," Johnny said.

I was surprised he said that. Couldn't see a reason for it. Surprised them too. Surprised them so much their mouths flew open.

Even Johnny looked surprised. "That startles you?" he said.

"No, no!" That was Darcie. "We're not startled," she says. "Course not. Just that we never met none of that kind before. Heard of you, of course. But we never been that way. Paw don't hold with Jaconi, seemingly. Though I don't know why. Never done no harm to him. Far as I know, anyway."

Yen's face suddenly burst into smiles.

"He's been funning us!" he hooted. "He's been pulling our leg! Jaconi knows all about the fire walking!"

The others nodded slowly, and Yen pounded his fist on the table. "Old Uncle Woofti's crazy in the head, like always," he hollered.

He turned to Johnny and spoke in a hoarse whisper, one eye on the door. "You know what that old rascal said?" he hissed. "You know what he said?"

"Shut up, Yen," Darcie muttered, and kicked him under the table.

"Hey! Don't do that!" he yelled. "You know I can't afford no bruises on my shins."

He turned back to Johnny, laughing so he could hardly talk. "He said... Old Uncle Woofti, he said... we was to get you to take up with little Darcie here, so's we could milk some good out of you. Pull the wool over your eyes— being as you're a prince and all..."

Darcie kicked again, but he paid no attention. "Jaconi!" he hooted. "And we was supposed to butter you up!"

"I'll get you, Yen," Darcie warned.

"Don't worry about her," Eson put in. "She's only a spitfire."

"I am not!"

"You sure enough spit fire the other day when them bloosie flames licked off your..."

"You hold you tongue, Eson Bent!"

"Don't make no difference!" Eson said, and grinned. "Jaconi knows. Your paw will sure be mad."

"Shut up, Eson," Yen said. "Darcie's right for once. I mean, a prince and all."

He took a pull at his drink and turned to Johnny. "So if you don't mind me asking, Prince," he said, "what the hell are you doing here? If I knew what you know, I'd be off in a cloud of dust."

"From time to time one of us has to travel on urgent business," Johnny said, like he knew what he was talking about. Even had me almost convinced.

"Yeah," Yen said. "Heard that. Supposed to be an old man loose in the hills right now. Comes and goes by magic, they say. Now you see him, now you don't. Never can tell where he'll turn up next."

"That's stupid!" Darcie snapped. "I don't believe a word of it."

"Well, I do," Eson hollered. "I seen him."

"Oh, you never did."

"Did too! You wasn't there. Seen him plain as day, sitting on a split-rail fence and playing with a kitten."

Darcie and Yen doubled up laughing.

"You never did see him!" Darcie hooted. "You made that up!"

"Did not!"

"Well, never mind," Darcie sighed. "We know what we know. Just enough to walk on fire and not get burnt. But you, Prince. You know a whole lot more than what we do, and you'd ought to..."

Yen kicked Darcie under the table. "Here comes Uncle Woofti," he muttered out of the side of his mouth.

Johnny bought them another round and we got out while the getting was good.

"I know what I know!" Eson was hollering, as we went through the door.

"They know what they know," Johnny muttered. "And they think they know what I know. I wish I did! Jaconi means something, and the higher you climb the more it means. But what!?"

"Don't ask me," I said. "I'm just along for the ride..."

Chapter: 2

I t's too far for you to start back to the city at this hour!" Alice was saying.

We're all standing on the doorstep of her house in Hawberry, and I gather she's been persuading Ern to stay the night. I also gather Ern doesn't need much persuading. She's getting a crick in her neck from looking at the stars, and she's hanging onto George when she feels giddy. Having the time of her life, in other words.

"Not all that far," I say. "With luck we'll make it before midnight."

Alice turns big, worried eyes on me. "And without luck?" she says.

I put an arm around her and gave her a squeeze.

"I want my children back where they belong," she whispers into my shoulder.

"Got an extra bunk at my place," George offers.

"You're a big help," I tell him, but I can see we're staying.

Alice brushes away a tear and gives me a kiss. "You'll make a wonderful married man," she whispers.

"And we'll take the kids back with us!" Ern is saying, like she just had a great idea. "They'll love Red Dragon Square. And that will give Alice a chance to pack in peace."

Didn't know what she figured I was going to pack in, but the faces all around closed the deal.

"Can we really?" Maudy says. "Can we, Auntie Ern? Can we ride in Johnny's car? He told me all about it one day we went home in the truck, and I remembered. Sometimes I play I'm a princess and ride in a big, white car with a white hat and a red coat."

"All right, then," I say. "Loading up early, though. Crack of dawn!"

Budd loaded up the pickup that day after the pancakes. "Come along then," he said. "You'll have to sit in the back with the kids and the dog. But if you've a mind to go to town, you're welcome."

We'd been sitting on the steps of the log cabin watching the sun burning mist off the rimrocks and sending long, fuzzy streamers into the valley.

"Sure would like to stay though," Budd said. "If there was a school up here..."

In the back of the truck, Maudy snuggled down beside Johnny, a gray woollen blanket wrapped around her and a bright green cap pulled over her ears. Long strands of red hair kept blowing around her head and getting into her eyes and mouth.

"I've got a cat," she said. "His name is Blinkey. And Bobby's got six chooks."

"They lay real good," Bobby said. "Ma says she couldn't do without them."

"Will you stay at our house?" Maudy suggested. "You can have one of Bob's eggs for breakfast, and I'll let you play with Blinkey."

"I'd like that," Johnny said. "I like cats."

I thought he was about to start in and tell her the story of that time when he was five. But his mind was on more exalted things, as the road snaked down the Moonstream gorge.

My first gorge. And it scared hell out of me! Wished to all the powers of heaven I was doing the driving myself. Switchbacks! Sheer drops! Tight bends! Loose gravel! And always, down below, the river, turquoise under the sun, deep and swift.

I tried to find a comfortable position for my legs. Couldn't do it. Tried to find a comfortable place for my eyes. Couldn't do that either— the truck bounced, and I had to see what was going on! And once, when Budd braked hard and we skidded on the gravel, I nearly had heart failure.

It was only a few dusty sheep though, that he came on suddenly around a bend.

I jumped down and chased them off the road. Strange sensation, being on my feet there. Felt about the size of an ant. Liked it, and didn't. But everybody took it for granted I could walk on that road and not fall off the edge.

After that I studied the steep, dry sides of the mountain. Didn't see what sheep would be doing there. Didn't see what they would find to eat. That was all I knew!

Later, deep into the gorge, with dark cliffs hanging over us, sometimes we passed under springs in the rock where the air was damp and cool. One of them sprayed me in the face and the kids nearly killed themselves laughing. They knew a city dude when they saw one.

"Our Uncle Janos wanted to go to the City once," Jack said. "Before he got lost. Down there."

He pointed down to the river, but I knew enough by then not to look.

Deeper, the wind howled and Maudy put her hands over her ears.

"...dry, old screaming... Dry, old screaming on the cold, old stones... And the ragged screaming..." Johnny muttered.

Hearing that I shuddered and the kids looked at me with wide, enquiring eyes.

But deep in Jaconi holy country with Johnny, nobody stirred. We watched him and saw through his eyes a little. Sort of made us feel we were part of the cliffs, of the green water, and of the long, slow descent. Long after we crossed the bridge and heard the tires take hold of the gravel for the long, slow climb back into sky and sun, we were still hushed...

Heading for George's extra bunk I heard my footsteps echo the way they do on boardwalks, and almost couldn't understand. Should have been hearing gravel crunch. Should have been able to look up and see rocks and snowfields between me and the stars, and down, to their reflection far below...

As the sun sank behind Maundy, we crossed over Heliope and ran along the rim of a deep bowl in her eastern flank. The river spread out in strands far below, and the lights of Hill City climbed the slopes on either side.

"Isn't it pretty?" Maudy said.

"A city set on a hill," Johnny murmured, and I shivered... Just about everything he said that day made me shiver.

"What did you say?" Maudy asked.

"Just some words from an old song," he told her, and smiled.

She thought about what he said and was quiet till Budd stopped the truck on a terrace high above the town. Then she took his hand.

"This is our house," she said. "You can get out now. We have to go inside and cook our supper."

So we climbed down, stiff and sore, and by the time we finished looking at the lights of the city below, Alice had a log fire blazing on the hearth and was running water into a copper pot.

"Plenty of room," Budd said. "You can bunk on the verandah with the boys. We'll eat now. Then I'll have to run Alice in to work. I don't let her out by herself at night if I can help it..."

Lying there in George's extra bunk, I thought of Ern out under the stars. And I thought of Alice... Hiding her tears from Budd. Thinking we might have an accident and she'd never get to the Meads, never get the kids out of harm's way, never see Budd smile again without a tired shadow in his eyes... Never walk away from some bar and wipe her hands on her apron for the last time.

I pictured Alice with the little round bag she used to carry her apron in to work. Wondered if she still had it. Hardly a day went by in Hill City that we didn't see that bag.

They were good days, for Johnny and me. Fell into a lazy pattern. The kids got up and clattered around the house till it was time to go to school. Maudy fed her cat. Bobby gathered the eggs from the hens' nests under the sleeping porch.

We slept. Ate. Wandered around town. Took care of the kids after school and through the evening. Sometimes we drove Alice to work, one or both of us—

Budd found a part-time job at the Loggers' Union Hall and worked odd hours.

One night we whistled up a dog and fastened him on a chain in the back of the pickup...

Alice sat between us. Didn't say much. Never did say much on the way to work. I couldn't help thinking of Ern and how she would react to a situation like Alice's, and I laughed.

"Just imagining Ern in Hill City," I explained.

"Ern would lay the place by the ears," Johnny said.

"I'd like to meet her someday," Alice murmured.

Didn't seem likely.

My mind went back to Ern and the Red Dragon. Went so far back I was surprised when we stopped in the yard behind the bar and I had to get down to let Alice out.

Watched her disappear between a dumpster and a pile of bottle crates. Watched till she was safe inside. Then Johnny started up the truck again and we rattled through a narrow alley. I remember a flowering creeper on a brick wall that was giving off a sickly smell and made me feel uneasy. Before I could roll up the window, some of it touched my hand. Felt sticky.

Along a dark street, then, and into a cobbled square behind the Loggers' Union. Budd was supposed to meet us there.

We sat in the cab with the windows down and listened to a brass band playing. A marching band, milling around the square like flies. In the middle, shifting colours played over a small stage where a contortionist was going through some tricks.

A lot of people stood around. Nobody was taking in the show though.

After a few minutes a skinny girl approached us, sometimes green sometimes purple as the lights changed. But the dog growled and she moved off. I started thinking about Missy.

The contortionist finished her act and a conjurer took her place. Dragged a few kittens and some old flags out of a carpet bag. Still nobody showed much interest.

A bum lurched up to the cab on my side and peered in at me. Reeking of acrite. Didn't say anything. Just stopped a minute, then shuffled across the square.

Budd came out of the Union.

Johnny turned the key.

And all of a sudden I'm leaping out of the truck and sprinting into this alley that opens off the square. My heart is thumping. Missy is going up that alley. I can see her, always keeping a few steps ahead of me.

Heard somebody running behind me, but that didn't seem out of the way, and I wasn't prepared for being tackled around the legs as I was starting up a set of stairs between two tall buildings.

"Hold on, mate," Budd hollers. "Where do you think you're going?"

I'm on this staircase. Steep. Rough. Some of the treads are broken. Grimy walls on either side. And one naked, yellow bulb on the first landing.

"What in hell are you doing?" I roar.

"Come on. Saloon Gulch is no place for the likes of you," Budd says. "This place'd make Red Dragon Square look like a Sunday School picnic. Come on. We'll get out of here. I'll take you someplace safe and buy you something to wash the pods out of you."

"But Missy," I blubber. "Missy. Missy, you bastard. Missy."

"Use your head," Budd says, while he's all the time trying to pull me back to the truck and I'm all the time pulling him up the steps.

"Nobody you know in Sally Alley," he says. "Sinkhole of sin! No place for you. And no place for a family man like me neither. Come on, before somebody spooks Johnny."

The mention of Johnny cleared my head a little, but by that time we were on the landing under the yellow bulb, and the same bum that looked into the truck at me lurches out of a doorway. The fumes of his breath are all around us. I'll swear his eyes glowed red.

I stood swaying, but Budd brought his big right fist up off the ground and hit the fellow under the chin as hard as he could. There's a crash as the bum strikes the door and bursts it open, and a lot more noise as Budd roars down the stairs dragging me behind him.

"What did you do that for?" I yell. "Poor, harmless, old..."

"Poor, maybe. Harmless, no. And not old neither, more than likely," Budd growls as he pulls me along.

The dog in the back of the truck is barking as we reach the square and Johnny has the motor running. Budd shoves me through a crowd that has gathered and raises his fist to a couple of shadowy figures between us and the cab door. Poured me in. Pushed me into the middle. And jumped in himself.

Johnny spun the wheels and we shot out of the square and up a steep street lined with lime-green lanterns— I think.

After awhile we're on a terrace high above the town, and Budd takes us through this ruin of crumbling stone onto a balcony overhanging a sheer drop to the river. Hill City is all around us.

Somebody brings me a cool drink in a clay mug. Tastes a bit like ginger, a bit like tea.

"Drink up," Budd says. That'll clear the pod juice out of you."

"What pod juice?" I hollered. "I never touch the stuff."

"All the more reason not to get too close then," he said, and laughed. "That old eater had you fair spooked."

"What in hell are you talking about?" I growled.

I guess I must have been looking pretty black. Anyway, Budd told me to keep my shirt on.

"This is a queer place, Hill City," he said, "and you just ran foul of one of our local traps. That eater was so full of pods one puff of his breath would put a youngun like you away for a week."

"What!?"

"That's how the miners in the back hills handle pain, you know," he told us. "Can't touch the stuff themselves. Addictive. Too dangerous in the pits. So when they need help they send for an eater, and pin their faith on him— or her. I thought you'd know."

"I knew the bargees smuggled the pure stuff upcountry," I said. "But I mean, we worked up to Wooji for the best part of a year and never saw..."

"I'm talking about back-country," Budd says. "Places like you've never seen. Eaters come high in there— no joke intended! And welcome. A broken leg or a crushed hand can hurt like hell."

"Did you know about all this?" I said to Johnny.

"We have our ways," he said, and grinned.

"Yeah? Well, you knew what that old eater was."

"Yes," he said, "but I got my information from books. I saw that man come up to the truck and look in at you, but..."

"Look in?" Budd snorted. "Puff in— by the way you took out after that skinny tart..."

"Skinny tart!" I roared.

I was on my feet without knowing how I got there and Budd was saying, "Sit down. That's what happens. Eater puffs you. You see something close to your thoughts at the moment. He lures you into some nice, dark corner... And the locals do the rest."

"Then... Thanks."

"You'd do the same for me," he said, and looked out over the town.

I turned to Johnny. I'm still shaking and trying to clear my head. "But Missy," I said. "She was..."

"No," he said.

He smiled and put a hand on my shoulder.

And suddenly I'm feeling fine. Better than fine. Terrific. Clean. Enjoying life. Quiet. Like after a sickness when you know you're better.

And just when I'm beginning to wonder why I'm feeling like this, Budd turns to Johnny and says, "You too. Not even your heathen necklet would save you if them eaters got you."

"So you've noticed that," Johnny said.

"Yeah. Heard of them," Budd answered. "And it beats me what you're doing here. First I took you for a log jockey looking for work, but that didn't last long. Then awhile back I saw the necklet. Well, it's no business of mine, but I never came across no young eaglet out of the nest before."

"That's well put," Johnny said, and laughed. "I'm out of the nest and trying to get back in."

"Well, spring's coming," Budd said. "Season when birds are on the lookout. Never can tell."

"My problem is," Johnny said, "I don't know where the nest is. Let alone how to get there..."

It was time for me to get back to the nest. Spring was coming again, and I needed clear mountain air, clean mountain water, space. Thought of that as I listened to George snore and planned the morning...

We had no plans for that late winter morning in Hill City, but I gathered my gear together. Didn't have to be told. Nobody did. Alice got up before daylight to make us breakfast, and Budd sat by the cold hearth and shivered. Maudy appeared dressed for outdoors. Even the boys came, but still in their pajamas.

"God go with you," Alice murmured, and kissed us.

After we shouldered our packs, Maudy took a hand of each of us and walked with us to the end of the street. Went as far as she dared from home, then stopped and took a small paper bag out of her pocket. It was her favourite bag that she used every day to carry her lunch to school, but she put it in Johnny's hand.

He took it and held it.

"Thank you, Maudy," he said. "But this is your lunch."

"I'll make another one."

"I wish I had something to leave with you," he said, "but all I have is a shadowy man who loves kids and kittens. If you watch for him, maybe you'll see him some day. He's not much to look at, but you'll like him. Tell him you're a friend of mine. He'll know."

Just then the sun rose over the rimrocks and flooded the terrace in misty light. We hugged our little friend and walked away.

When I looked back for the last time, she was still standing where we left her, gazing into the rising sun. Not moving. But Alice was coming to get her.

I guess she heard her mother coming, because she turned and called out, "He did, Mother! I think He did!"

"He did?" Alice echoed.

"Yes, He did! You said it, and He did."

"What, darling?" Alice called. "What did I say?"

"To go with them, Mother," Maudy shouted. "To go with them. God, Mother! You said, 'God go with them', and He did! Didn't you see Him? He was shining right beside them, and Johnny saw Him too."

There was a light powdering of snow in the shadows...

Enormous pink roses grew out of a snowbank by my back door. I could hardly get out of the house for them.

Smallest Granddaughter's geese honked. Sounded like ten-ton trucks.

A cold wind off the snowfields blew over me.

"Come on, come on," George hollered, as he pulled my blanket off. "Going to town this morning. Didn't forget, did you? Budd and me are taking the truck in too. Come on. Time we hit the road."

It was time for Maudy's dream to come true, too. Ern sat in back with the boys and Maudy sat in front with me, every inch a princess in a red coat and a white hat.

Red Dragon Square will remember Maudy's visit for a long time. As for me, even showing the kids the sights with Ern, sometimes my mind went back to the mountains, and sometimes I didn't hear what anybody said to me.

"Never mind," Ern told Maudy one morning down by the canal when she asked me the same question three times, "he's only planning ahead. He wants everything to be ready for our trip."

I wasn't thinking much about this trip, though— more about the other one.

"Sorry, Maudy," I said. "I was thinking about Johnny."

"That's all right then," she told me. "What were you thinking?"

"Remember Oomiskaya?"

"Tell me."

"Well, it was that first day after we left Hill City...

We were high in the rimrocks, climbing into an orange sunset. I was keeping my eye on Johnny's shape against the sky, and my chest was begging for the day to end.

Nothing moved up there. Nothing but us. And near the top of this narrow pass, Johnny stopped moving too. My whole body thanked him. Sitting down up there was about the most welcome thing I ever did.

We were on this narrow ledge under a slight overhang. And three steps to the side, the mountain fell off into nothing.

Nothing!

I wedged my back into a crack in the rock and shut my eyes.

But Johnny...

"Freedom!" he says, filling his lungs deep. "Freedom, all around. Will you look at those valleys soaring up the sides of the peaks?"

"I can see them," I muttered.

"Open your eyes!" he says, and gives me a poke that nearly knocks me off the ledge.

"That's infinity out there!" he hollers.

"If you say so."

He's laughing and I know how his eyes are sparkling without having to see them.

"This is where the mountains fall into flight," he says. "Sky. Space. Look at it!"

"I'll take your word for it," I tell him, and I try to push myself farther into the rock.

"Come on," he says, and gives me another punch on the shoulder. "Open your eyes!"

"They're open," I'm saying.

Then I choke.

I'm looking.

And what I'm seeing is this big fawn cat flowing down the ledge.

Didn't dare move.

Couldn't even whisper.

Johnny's sitting there, gazing out into the sky with all the happiness in the world in his face. And I can't even warn him.

After a minute he raises his canteen and takes a drink.

The cat's ears twitch.

Johnny reaches into his pocket and takes out your lunch bag, Maudy, and holds it in his hands.

The tip of the cat's tail lifts.

Then Johnny reaches into the bag and takes out a sandwich. Held it out to me, actually.

My mouth opened, but I couldn't make a sound.

The cat raised his muzzle and sniffed.

Well, Johnny could tell by my face, then, that there was something behind him.

"Don't move," I tried to say, but I was petrified! By that time the cat was swinging down the trail of peanut butter! Johnny was catching on though.

Slowly he turned, with the sandwich in his hand.

The cat stopped.

Four or five yards up the pass he stopped and watched our every move, just the end of his tail twitching.

Johnny smiled.

"Howdy, marshall," he whispered. "Riding your boundaries, are you? I've been looking for you. It's been a long time. Going to run us off? Or remember me and let us be?"

The cat blinked.

Johnny never took his blue eyes off those yellow ones, but he reached out as far as he could and put the sandwich on the ground between them.

The smell of peanut butter hung all around us, and the cat's tongue came out and licked the air.

He stretched. He looked out over the valley like he had no other interests in life; like he didn't even know we were there. Then he padded on down the ledge with his tail swaying.

"Help yourself," Johnny told him. "Join us. Maudy would be delighted."

The cat watched him, but he stretched out his nose to the sandwich... And it was gone! Vanished!

Johnny gave him another one. That vanished too.

That cat ate every one, Maudy. All Johnny and I had of your lunch was half each of your big red apple!

But I was breathing again.

And Johnny... He was looking... Well, I don't think there's a word for it, but if there is, it means very, very happy— as happy as anybody can be and not burst.

So was the cat— looking very happy, as far as I could tell. Anyway, as soon as he saw there wasn't any more to eat but apple core, which he doesn't like, he settled down with his head on his paws and looked us over.

I would have given a lot to know what he made of us. I mean, beside him I felt pretty awkward and puny. He was beautiful, Maudy— but you'll see him. This tawny brown colour. Sleek. No scars. Perfect! And he was between us and the way we wanted to go!!

Well, I was glad Johnny wasn't making any move to push his way by— not being acquainted with Oomi at the time— so I breathed a little easier and looked around a bit.

It was beautiful up there on the rimrocks. Thin and peaceful. The sun was sinking and light was flowing up the slopes. I never knew light flowed before. Almost like water. I was surprised, but Oomi knew all about it, and what it meant to us. Rest time.

His head settled heavier on his paws.

His ears relaxed.

His eyes blinked once or twice.

And he purred.

He purred!

"Thanks, marshall," Johnny says, very quiet. "Appreciate the welcome."

"That's goes for me too, pussy," I croaked. "Don't forget I said so too."

So, having introduced ourselves, the three of us sat there, resting, for quite a long time.

Later, when the moon cleared the peaks across the way, Johnny reached for his pack and we started up the pass— all three of us...

"I'll like Oomi," Maudy said. "Will Oomi like me?"

"Sure to," I said. "Specially if you make him sandwiches. And speaking of sandwiches... Ern?"

"You're right," Ern agreed. "Must be time for lunch. Let's stop in at Andy's and treat the kids to squiggy buns. And while we're eating you can tell us... Oh! There's one of those mountain sling-bags in that stall. What do you think? Just a minute till I see."

So while Ern shopped, the kids and I strolled along the street toward Andy's, but I tramped in the hills.

Chapter: 3

I don't know how long we travelled after that sunset in the rimrocks. I only remember golden days and silver nights. Winter on the peaks and spring in the valleys. And walking. Always walking. But my legs were coming under me and I wasn't needing so much rest. Or thought. My head turned off in favour of my thighs and I just enjoyed moving.

Then one evening I looked around and realized we were swinging down into a wide green valley, forested below, grassed on the upper slopes. The moon sparkled on patches of snow and a stream ran beside us through meadows of columbine and day lilies. Beyond the valley, in the far distance, a massive range reared up. And from the green slope above the trees, every once in awhile we caught sight of a ribbon of road leading that way.

We made for that road and struck it on a morning of cold drizzle. Couldn't see the peaks for cloud and mist, but judging by the wind that scraped our faces, they weren't far ahead.

The country was bleak, the air was thin and sharp, and the wind sighed in dry brown grasses all that day.

A stream beside the road ran shallow in the early hours, deep and swift by afternoon. Sometimes the roar was so loud we couldn't hear each other speak. Once Johnny stopped and held up his hand. I froze and listened. Over the noise of the river I could just make out a deep rumble.

"Must be a big waterfall," I shouted.

"Avalanche," he said, and his face lit up.

Lord love us! I would have settled for a nice pair of mudsharks...

Speaking of mudsharks, Ern and I and the kids were all sitting in Andy's sidewalk cafe by that time, admiring Ern's new sling bag and polishing off fresh strawberry buns.

"We won't have time to cook anything tonight either," Ern was saying, "so we'll take home some fish and chips and get on with the packing. Kids like fish and chips."

"They never tasted fish like you get here," I told her. "Nothing to compare with it up to Hill City where they come from. You better eat your fill too. You won't get mudshark where you're going."

That seemed to give her pause for thought as they say.

"And remind me to get on my knees to Andy and see if he won't give me the recipe for squiggy buns," I said. "We have a great baker up the Meads, but we can't seem to get the mix quite right."

"I'll get it for you," Ern said. "Soon's we finish eating I'll take Maudy back to the kitchen. She'll melt old Andy's heart... Good strawberries up the Meads, are there?"

"The best," I said. "Smallest Granddaughter picks them for us."

"Who's smallest granddaughter?" Maudy wanted to know. "Is she smaller than me?"

"You'll meet her in the mountains, Maudy," I said.

So while Ern and Maudy went back to see Andy, and the boys ran out to the street to watch a fellow on a monocycle, I sat in the heat of Red Andy's cafe and shivered in the wind blowing off a glacier in a high cirque.

Snow was coming. A thin mist already blurred the peaks, and a strange, mustard-coloured light shone everywhere. Rags of the mist drifted across the road, thicker the farther we went. I didn't like it, but Johnny kept on ahead like he could see right through it.

Suddenly, around a bend, we came to a village. Didn't seem possible, but there it was. Six tiny houses, looking like they grew right out of the side of the mountain, and some stems of straw blowing down the street ahead of a strong wind. I could smell something too— animals.

"What's that smell?" I said to Johnny. I mean, I've come across a lot of smells in my time, but nothing like that.

He laughed at me. "Goats," he said.

I shrugged. Well... It takes all kinds...

What surprised me most was that nobody saw us coming. You'd think somebody would've at least peeked out a window. But we got right through the village and up the far end before we saw any sign of life. Up there though, in front of the last, low house, right where the cliff curved and moisture dripped down a runnel out of the clouds, there was this old bus, standing still, icing over.

A gray old sign out in front of the building was swaying back and forth. I couldn't read the writing, but Johnny said, "Bakery."

That sounded good to me.

We went closer. Still no sign of life though. No bread smell. Nobody in sight. Only the bus standing there.

Johnny pushed open the door and we looked inside.

The minute we did that, smoke started pouring out and a dull, smouldering fire flared up in the fresh air we brought in. In the middle of the shop two men were struggling. I thought at first they were fighting.

One of them had to be the bus driver. The other one was a big fellow in a white apron.

The bus driver was a lot smaller than the baker and his muscles were bulging with the effort he was putting out. I thought the baker must be trying to murder him or something, but then I saw that the driver was trying to get the baker into a chair and the baker was flinging his arms around like he wanted to get rid of his hands. Sometimes he'd hug them to his chest. Then he'd fling them out to the side. And all the time he kept yelling but making no sense.

Then there's this little voice from behind us. "Pappa!" she's saying. "Pappa!"

Neither of us noticed this little girl trembling behind the door before.

"The fire," she said. "The oven broke and the fire came through. And he put his hands..."

At that moment the baker flung his hands wide again and one of them struck the windowledge.

"For God's sake, help!" the bus driver hollered. "I can't hold him."

I jumped in and got hold of one arm, the driver held the other, and we got the baker into the chair under the window. But not for long. He sort of hung between us for a minute. Then he passed out and we had to let him down onto the floor. We tried to do it so he wouldn't hurt his hands again, but he wasn't feeling anything anyway.

Johnny had his arms around the little girl, holding her back, and she was crying, "Poor Pappa! Poor Pappa!"

For a minute we all stood looking down at the baker.

Then the little girl said to Johnny, "I could bring some baking soda."

He only smiled at her. But there was this powerful feeling in the room. I thought it was sympathy, at first. Then I didn't know... Then I was sure it wasn't.

I mean, I started out thinking, "Poor kid, she's scared to death. She's almost as white as her pappa's apron."

But pretty soon— I mean, right away, I'm thinking, "What am I talking about!? This is no poor kid. I don't know when I've seen a prettier little girl. Not with eyes like those. And rosy cheeks..."

And then this smile comes out from behind her eyes, and we're all smiling.

"What about the oven?" Johnny asks her.

"Oh!" she says. "It's full of coals and the shop will burn down! Oh, sir!"

So the two of them ran into the back room and the bus driver and I watched from the doorway.

It was very smoky in there and the heat was already charring the ceiling beams, but Johnny looks at the child. "What should we do?" he says.

She told him... This. And this. And that. And that's what he did, like he did that sort of thing every day. And when he's finished, he looks surprised we're all watching him with our mouths open.

But even he was surprised when we went back into the front room and there's the baker sitting in the chair under the window holding his hands up to his eyes. They weren't black and swollen any more, and you could see by his face the pain was gone.

The little girl's eyes flew to Johnny.

"He put his hands in the fire," she said. "Pappa put his hands in the fire. Oh, sir! He put his hands in the fire!"

She stuck her own hands behind her back, and backed up against her father's knee for good measure...

Maudy came back from Andy's kitchen and cuddled up on my knee.

"I was telling you about that, Ern, wasn't I?" I said.

"What? she asked. "You must have a touch of the sun or something. You haven't told me anything. I been..."

"I didn't tell you about the fire?"

"No."

I shook my head.

"Come on," she said. "You've been sitting here long enough. Andy's going to write out the recipe and have it for us tomorrow. Time we were..."

"And I wasn't telling you about the day Johnny and the bus driver..." I muttered, as I stood up.

"No. Now where are those boys?! Oh. Come on you two."

She grabbed Maudy by the hand and started up the Square herding the two boys ahead of her.

"That was George, of course," she said to me over her shoulder. "The bus driver? You'll have to tell me later."

Still shaking my head, I followed her and her family up the Square, that was full of the afternoon crowd by that time.

Some kids got into a fight, which took everybody's attention for a few minutes, but a cop blew a whistle and we moved on. A fish cart pushed by and Bobby started putting the questions to me about mudsharks and other attractive life forms. And Jack almost got lost, his attention being snapped when a cute little redhead selling baskets suggested he might like to buy one for his mamma...

The Square was hot, crowded, and noisy. But I was seeing it like I was seeing it through a cold, misty little window...

Of course all the people crowded into the bakery and stared at us. Before long I was feeling like a lion in a cage. But George took over proceedings.

"Be snow tomorrow," he said. "The road'll be closed. But soon as it melts off a bit I'll take you down. Be glad to."

"We've come up from the valley," Johnny said.

Well, that surprised their eyes open! First they looked at us. Then they looked out the little window under the eaves. You couldn't see anything but black night out there by then, but the mind's eye can always see things, and they knew what would be there. I didn't, of course. I mean, I'd never seen snow scudding ahead of a wind before. Or deep drifts. Or ice glittering overhead on sharp rock ridges. I knew they were seeing things like that, but I couldn't see them myself, yet.

Just then a gust slid around the house and stirred the smell of the fire.

"We could maybe get to Sindabardi," George said. "If the snow holds off past Penner's Rock, and the fords of The Races aren't flooded... We could maybe make it... Maybe. Maybe not."

"I don't expect anyone to come with me," Johnny said.

"No. But better than going up afoot," George says. "And faster in the long run, though not by much."

"Could you get back?" I asked.

"Oh, no trouble getting back," he says. "Never no trouble getting back. It'll be getting up that's hard..."

I kept thinking about that remark of George's all the time Ern was arguing with the fish and chips seller, off and on while we all walked up the alley, and even while we ate, sitting around the kitchen table and digging in like we hadn't been eating squiggy buns half the afternoon.

Sometimes I was there with Ern and the kids. Sometimes I wasn't.

At last my head cleared and I realized the sun was gone down and the evening was cooling off.

Supper was not cleared away and the smell of fish was strong in the room.

Ern was leaning on her elbows. Maudy was cuddled up on my knee again. And even the boys were both there listening with all their ears.

Judging by my throat, I'd been talking all through the meal and afterward. Couldn't remember what I'd been telling them, but I must have been making a good story of it. Guess it had something to do with trouble going up but not coming back, because Ern was looking worried.

"I certainly hope it won't be hard getting up this time," she said. "George never mentioned trouble."

"Will it, Arnold?" Bobby asked. He was looking a little scared too.

"Of course not," I said. "We know the way now. Didn't Johnny go up and find it for us?"

"Did he?"

"Well, I'm telling you," I said, "and all I get is interruptions, interruptions, interruptions!"

I wasn't sure of my ground when I said that, but Maudy laughed and snuggled closer. "Tell me about the little girl," she said. "Was she Smallest Granddaughter?"

So I was making sense to her at least.

"Which little girl was that?" I asked, real innocent. Knew I was taking a chance.

"The one in the bakery!" she said, as if I should have known. "Don't you remember?"

"Oh!" I said. "That little girl! No, that was Tassie. She's the one that helped the grandmother bring us fresh rolls and hot milk and honey in the morning. Tasted real good."

"I like milk and honey," Maudy said.

But my head was up in the high hills again...

The snow had held off so far, but the wind was very cold, and heavy cloud hung over the rooftops.

Everybody gathered to see us off. They came out of the houses wrapped up in coats and shawls, and stamped their feet to keep them warm. Didn't say anything to stop us, but they looked like they wouldn't give much for our chances.

"There'll be drifts under Penner's Rock," an old man told me as I came out. "You'll have to dig her through."

"He's a strong young fellow!" his old wife snapped. "And snow's better than flooding in The Races! No man can shovel water!"

"Now if you only had one of them fancy plough blades," somebody else said. "Too bad George never had a plough."

George was coming out behind me.

"We could've sailed right on to Medalsring, if we had a plough," he said in a big, booming voice.

A hush fell, and some of the people made a sign in the air with their fingers.

"You oughtn't to talk loud of that place," the old lady whispered. "Least not when he's about."

"You be respectful, George," they said. "And don't tempt fate. How'd you like to spend the rest of the winter buried under Penner's Rock?"

George laughed and went on out to the bus with a sheepskin coat slung over his shoulder by one finger. He pulled open the door and climbed into the driver's seat. After a minute the engine caught with a rattle and a blast of black smoke...

"Tell me about the smallest granddaughter, Arnold," Maudy said. "I've been asking you and asking you. Is she smaller than me?!"

She sounded like she was getting a little cranky. Time for bed, I guess.

"I was just trying to decide how to tell you the next bit, Maudy," I said.

"Yes, but you take too long," she complained. "Just tell me."

"Well, all right," I say. "Patience, patience..."

I'm standing out in front of the baker's house, all ready to go— it's still early in the morning— when out comes Johnny with the grandmother and Tassie. Tassie is carrying a great big sheepskin coat for him.

And behind them comes this even smaller granddaughter, and she's tripping over the sleeves of an even bigger sheepskin coat.

"This one is for you," she says, looking up at me. "But you'll have to put it on yourself, 'cause I can't lift it... You could lift me though."

I put on the coat and showed her how it looked. Then I lifted her up so she was looking down on all the people round about. Her head was almost in the clouds.

She gave me a hug. "Your name is Arnold," she said. "I haven't got a name yet, so you have to call me Smallest Granddaughter. Will you come back again?"

"You can come and see me," I said. "When we get settled, George will bring you on the bus."

Maudy was pretty sleepy by then, but she was awake enough to mutter, "Did he?"

"Did who? What?"

"Oh, Arnold," she scolded. "Are you thinking again!? Did Smallest Granddaughter go to visit you on the bus!?"

"Of course," I said. "She lives up the Meads now, doesn't she. George brought the whole family when the winter was over, and they stayed. Who did you think made bread for us? Me?"

She giggled. "No," she said. "I don't think you can make bread. You can't even scramble chooks' eggs."

That was a reference to the time the chooks got out when I was cooking lunch for the kids up to Hill City. We all ran around the neighbourhood chasing hens while the eggs burned and ruined Alice's frying pan.

"Some things should never be remembered, Maudy Atherton," I said.

"It just shows you never know," Ern sighed. "Who'd have thought... I guess there was just the two of you going up that first time."

"Three," I said, "counting Oomi. He came bounding down onto the road from somewhere up in the mist at the last minute and followed us into the bus. Wasn't sure he liked it but wasn't going to be left behind. Didn't know what to make of us in sheepskin coats either, but he settled down at the back and spent the time twitching his ears and thumping the dust out of the seat with his tail."

"That must have taken a rise out of George," Ern said.

"Never turned a hair," I told her.

"Tell us about it," Maudy demanded.

"Well," I said, "Johnny settled into the seat right behind George. But you couldn't talk. Too noisy.

"After awhile, though, George motions for us to look ahead. And there's this big outcrop of rosy, crystalline rock. Huge thing. Colour of burnt out coals, because of the mist. But real pretty.

"Penner's Rock,' George shouted. 'That's where we'll meet the snow.'

"What's Penner's Rock?' Johnny shouted back."

I stopped, remembering...

"So what's Penner's Rock?" Ern prompts.

"Rose quartz," Jack tells her. "Almost pure. Biggest deposit in the world. Dad used to truck slabs of it down here for awhile."

"Of course! Gihon Square!" she hollers. "Remember, Arnold? That must be the stuff those arches are made of! Well, will you think of that! And Budd actually brought it down?"

"Some of it," Jack said. "It's very heavy so you can only take a slab or two at a time. But Dad says, now the new road is in it's not too bad."

"I never would have believed it!" Ern hooted.

"Are you two going mining rose quartz now?" I said. "Or am I telling you a story?"

"You go right ahead, honey," Ern says, and smirks at me. "We're all ears, aren't we, kids? Well... all except Maudy. She'll have to hear the story some other time."

I looked down at Maudy and smiled. Dead to the world. But the boys were still hanging on my every word.

"Used to be a town here,' George told us," I said. 'When the mine was working all the time. Fashionable once, you know. Ladies' gewgaws. Little bowls. Stuff like that... The Ebrit kings used to be buried in coffins made of Penner's quartz..."

"Yeah!" Bobby cried. "Me and Jack went to see them once. 'Member, Jack? All these creepy coffins down in the cellar?"

"That was Hill City Town Hall," Jack explained, for Ern's benefit.

"That's right," I said. "Johnny and I went there too. There's a lot of Penner's rock in the old Town Hall."

"Oh, yeah!" Bobby said, "Me and Jack and..."

"But you did, I believe," I complained, real dignified, "ask me to tell you what George intimated to us on the day in question?"

They giggled.

"So are you listening or going to bed!?"

They were about as scared of me as they'd be of an old dog with no teeth, but Bobby very kindly patted my arm and said, "We like your stories, Arnold. What did George say?"

"Miners cleared out when the bottom fell out of the market," George bellowed. "Can't blame them. Valley looks a pretty sight from up here, looking down."

"You stay," Johnny roars back.

"Yes. But when your jeans are frozen to a granite block, a nice soft cushion in the city looks pretty good sometimes," George argued.

"Not to me," Johnny says.

"Not to me though," George says.

Half the time they couldn't hear each other. Me, now. Across the aisle, wishing they'd shut up so I could get some sleep, I heard every word.

"That's why I took this job with the bus line," George says. "So I could live up here where I belong. Now and again I like to get down where the living's easy though..."

"That why he came down with you this time?" Jack wanted to know.

"Who?"

"George."

"Oh. No," I said, "he came because I bought a ticket on the Sindabardi bus. But I don't think he minded. Stayed up in Hawberry though, till he saw how things were turning out. Wouldn't be in town now if your dad wasn't here to do the driving. George knows when he's onto a good thing."

Ern was looking interested. "So finish what he was telling you about Penner's Rock," she said.

"Yes. Well, he says— or rather he hollers over the noise of the bus... 'Took the last of the miners down two, three years ago. Two old codgers been up here since they was nippers. Stayed on after the rest of the quartzers went away. Working the gold out of the rubble dumps. Thought they had the world by the tail when I picked them up."

He laughed and shook his head.

"Heard they never lasted a week in town,' he hollered. "Some accie puffed them, like as not. Takes time to get used to city ways. Don't do to take things fast..."

Ern was looking thoughtful, and I stopped to wonder if I was taking things too fast in the other direction. Had a feeling I might be. Didn't seem to be much I could do about it though.

"So just about then the first big fat flakes of snow splattered against the windshield," I said.

I figured that would be a good place to stop for the night. We'd get the kids to bed— at least the two little ones— and clear up the place a bit. But Bobby was still with us.

"Just finish this part," he said, "and then we'll go."

Ern agreed. She was interested too— any story with George in it.

So I grinned ear to ear and caught myself at it. Thought of Missy and felt a momentary flutter in the stomach.

"Oh, well. All right, then," I said, "I'm nearly done anyway," and I took a deep breath.

"I wiped the window beside me and peered out," I said. "Nothing to see but swirling mist and deep pits in the ground."

"Hand work," George roared. "No machines. Some say if you look close you can still see them working and hear them holler when the blocks let go."

Johnny smiled.

"Me, I never believed that," George went on. "Only the wind in the rocks... Sometimes that sounds like all the pipes of Hell let loose. But then I never been to Hell, yet. So how would I know?

"Never been to Medalsring either, for that matter," he says. "Though I may go some day... Heard a rumour we might get a party of three for the Meads this spring. But I'll believe that when I see it... Need a road first, for one thing."

Then he looks back at us kind of funny, like maybe, counting Oomi, we might be that party of three. Shook his head though. Told me later he changed his mind and didn't think so, then.

Johnny didn't say anything, and I looked out the window at the streams of snow swirling in the pits and blowing off the rubble dumps. Lots of snow. But no ghostly miners...

"I don't believe in ghosts," Maudy said, and I jumped like one just snuck up behind me and rammed its hands down the back of my neck.

"I thought you were asleep!" I hollered.

The boys laughed, but they looked like they maybe did— believe in ghosts, I mean— or would like to.

"Well, the road got steeper after that," I said, "and the bus made too much noise, even for George. So I got some sleep. And that's exactly what you're going to get right now. End of the line!" and I lifted Maudy to carry her to bed.

"That's what George says," Jack told me. "End of the line! All out for Sindabardi!"

"So he does."

When I came to think of it, that's what he said that night he took us up. "End of the line!" But I wasn't starting into that, not after a full day.

"So to quote George," I said, "this is definitely the end of the line for this day."

I carried Maudy, Ern brought Bobby with an arm around his shoulders, but Jack stayed behind in the kitchen.

"You too, Jack," I called.

"OK," he said. But he didn't appear, and when I went back for him, I found him staring out the kitchen door with the excuse of a drink of water in his hand.

When he turned he was very sober, but he smiled at me. "Thanks, Arnold," he said. "We're having a great time with you and Auntie Ern. I'll always remember it... Guess Bobby will too... But maybe not Maudy. She's pretty young."

"Long as she doesn't forget Ern and me, and squiggy buns, and telling stories, she'll be fine," I said, "and we'll see that she doesn't forget those things because we'll all be up the Meads together."

"Guess you're right," he said. "Good-night."

I staggered out the back and stretched out on my bed with all my clothes still on. Didn't even throw Cranky's cover over him. Figured I'd do that later.

Laid there thinking about the trip ahead and getting it all mixed up with the other one. Thinking of Missy and wondering if she'd care, one way or the other, when I showed up. Thinking of Cally, and Maudy, and Smallest Granddaughter...

Just thinking... remembering... dozing off... when the kitchen door opened and closed very carefully and somebody started toward the sleepout making very little noise. Raised up on one elbow just as Jack appeared in the doorway.

"Arnold?" he whispered.

"Come in," I said, and sighed.

Found the energy to move my feet so he could perch on the end of the bed, and laid back.

Cranky opened one eye and kind of mewed. He likes Jack. Maudy and Bobby, now, they keep a respectful distance and Cranky pretends he never sees them, but Jack can stroke his feathers and hold him on his wrist like he was a canary bird.

"Hi, C.B.," Jack said, being friendly— always calls him C.B..

I almost dozed off again, but then Jack turns to me and says, "Arnold? Are you awake? I have a couple of things to ask you. Had to wait till the little kids were asleep. Didn't want to worry them."

"There's nothing to worry about, Jack," I said.

"No, but I just wondered... I mean, I'm the oldest... Do you really think..? I mean..."

"Out with it," I said. "What's on your mind?"

"I'm wondering about my mother," he says then, real fast. "Do you think she'll be all right in Medalsring, Arnold? Do you think she'll like it there? And live to be an old lady— maybe forty-five?"

"More like eighty-five, Jack," I said. "And she'll like it. She wants to go."

"Oh, yes! We all want to go," he says, with this big smile. "Even Auntie Ern. And she's never been away from Red Dragon Square before."

"Ern, especially, wants to go," I said. "But that's not surprising. She's been ready for a long time— even if she didn't know it herself."

"Yes, but..."

"You see, Jack, nobody goes to Medalsring till they want to. Really want to. And I can tell you it's a great place, even for old ladies like Alice. I mean, wait till you see the grandmother!"

"Well, that's a load off my mind," Jack says, with a sigh, and my eyes close of their own accord.

But he's still sitting on the end of my bed, not making any move to leave.

"Did you say you had a couple of things to ask me?" I suggested, but without opening my eyes.

"Yeah," he agreed. "The other thing was C.B. We're taking him too... In his cage?"

"Cranky's staying in his cage right now for two reasons, Jack," I said. "First, because I want to be able to put my hand on him when the time comes, and not have to start looking for him at the last minute. Second, because some... person..."

"Bastard' is the word you usually use," he told me, with a big grin.

"Ok. But you're too young to use it. Remember that!"

"Oh, I don't!" he said. "At least, not out loud. Ma would skin me alive. But some... one of them..."

"Yes. Some one of them has been taking pot shots at Cranky. Winged him once or twice. Can't be a very good shot, whoever he is— which is a good thing for us. But one of these days his aim may improve. Therefore Cranky is tied up just now. But not for long."

"If he comes with us, he'll have to travel in his cage," Jack said.

"Yes, but he'll go free when we stop at night. If he wants to come back, he will. He's smart enough to find us out there— even if we move on without him."

"Would it... Would you mind... I mean, I know he's yours and all... But..."

"No," I said. "He's not mine. No more than I'm his. I used to think he was, but I found out different one day... Johnny taught me."

"Yeah?"

"Yeah. But don't sound so enthusiastic. Not tonight."

"No. But someday?"

"Sure. Just not now. I'm going to need my voice in a week or so— when I get up to Canalhead. Sure hope I have it left."

"Ok," Jack said, "I'm going. I just thought... I could look after C.B. for you... On the trip. Maybe help out a little..."

"Great idea!" I said. "It's a deal."

Cranky fluffed his feathers and squawked.

"He wants his blanket on," I muttered.

"And his water dish is nearly empty," Jack said. "I'll get him some."

I closed my eyes...

And Johnny strolled up the alley.

"Where you been?" I said.

"Around."

Cranky opened his beak and shrieked.

"Yeah, well," I said, "I was looking for you. Thought you might like a drive out to Port Island with me. Nice day for a drive."

"Sure," he agreed. "It's a nice day for a drive out to Port Island. What's going on out there? Church picnic? Girls softball game? Whimmydiddle contest?"

I reached into my shirt pocket and took out one of the blue- lightning pellets they give fighting birds. Held it on the palm of my hand. Cranky pounced on it and his crest blushed rosy from the bottom, then faded out to the usual golden green.

"Oh," Johnny says. "Going to the bird fights, are we?"

"You ever been?"

"No."

"Education for you."

"I didn't know bird fights were still going on," he said.

"There's a lot you don't know," I told him.

"But you do."

"Well, it's no great wonder, is it," I said. "I mean, you never grew up dockside like I did."

"No, but I used to wish I could," he said. "Was it fun?"

"No! Yes, of course it was! Just watch yourself, when we get there. What I mean... be careful."

We parked in a mechanic's lot at the edge of the island and walked in. Couldn't trust the roads. Or the bridges.

As we were crossing a rotting causeway, I gave Cranky another one of the blue pellets. Then I turned out my pocket and threw the crumbs into the canal. Not supposed to have them— but everybody did..

Johnny watched the stir as they struck the water.

"Remember not to fall in there," I said. "Those eels will be standing up and gnashing their teeth all night."

He gave me a funny look then, that I didn't understand till later.

"We have to go to the square in front of the St. Sier Mission," I said. "Then we walk west till we come to a broken bridge in about five minutes. Somebody will meet us there."

"How do you know?"

"Met a fellow somewhere," I said. "You leave that part of the proceedings to me. You're only second in command of this show, told off to form the rearguard."

"Aye, aye, sir. Cap'n Grieve, sir."

"Don't be cute," I said, "or I'll feed you to the birdie."

I stroked Cranky's head. He wouldn't bite me. But he was nervous, and he shrieked when this girl, about eleven or twelve, dropped out of a kiri tree behind us.

"That Cranky?" she asked.

"This is him," I said.

"Don't he wear a hood?"

"Naw," I said, "but I'll put his leash on him if he worries you."

"Me!?" she says. "I ain't worried. But you better hood him before he sees them others."

"That bad, are they?" I snapped back.

But all I got from her was a dirty look as she led us to this silted up old barge behind a rotting factory.

"In there," she said, and disappeared.

Inside there were three men in the circle. Full house, with me in...

One of these days I'll have to tell Jack about that meet, which I don't like remembering any more.

"You see, Jack," I'll have to say, "there were these three men squatting around this large bamboo cage in the bottom of the barge, under a spot where they'd torn out some of the decking to make a light-hole.

"I took the last place. Johnny squatted behind me in the second circle, where he could watch my back. There was sure to be money on this fight. Not a safe situation!

"The birds were hooded, all but Cranky. That was good. The others would go into the cage blind because of their hoods coming off at the last minute. Cranky would be in top form.

"Well, the initiator raised his right hand, this woman crept out from behind him with the sacrifice— these four small cubes of bloody meat on a saucer, and the birds strained against their leashes.

"There was a lot of shrieking, the bits of meat went down whole, and we all pushed our birds through these one-way ports in the basket.

"Cranky whistled, lifted himself on his wings... and broke the neck of the bird on his left. When he did that, his crest flooded with bright blue light. Never seen it before or since.

"The other birds circled the cage, keeping their beaks toward Cranky.

"Then one of them hesitated. It was no more than a missed step, but it was enough. Cranky struck again.

"Only one bird left— a young one from the upper delta— and he didn't know what to do. Just kept shuffling around the cage.

"Cranky seemed to swell. His breast feathers ruffled till you could see the down underneath, blazing like summer wildfire, and it was all over. Till Johnny leapt!

"One powerful swing from the shoulder and he swept the top right off the cage.

"Well, Jack," I'll say, "Cranky didn't even stop to think. Just lifted into the air, light as a bubble.

"For a second he hung over the barge with his talons down, like he was deciding whether to shake the dust of the place off his feathers then, or take a dive through the crowd first. The people were all packed in, and I think he figured some of them needed to lose a pint or two of blood before he left!

"But I ran for the gangway yelling, and sprinted along the pathway under the trees with Johnny coming right behind me.

"For a few wingbeats Cranky followed us. Then he floated away on an updraft of air. The last we knew of him was this long, piercing wail..."

Funny how sad I was to lose Cranky. And angry too. Could have killed Johnny. So after we left Port Island far behind and my heart stopped hammering, I turned on him and yelled, "What in hell did you do that for?!"

"Thought I would," he said.

I'll tell Jack that much. But I won't tell him Johnny looked at me afterward, in that way he has, and said, "Round and round. Round and round. And always left to right." That would take too much explaining.

But I'll say to Jack, "Johnny bought Cranky his freedom that day, and he's ours now only if he wants to be. Only if he wants to accept our food and water. Only if he can be our friend and neighbour..."

Jack came back then with Cranky's dish washed out and filled with fresh water. Stood and watched the bird drink a minute, then covered the cage with my old bush shirt.

Jack came back then with Cranky's dish washed out and filled with fresh water. Stood and watched the bird drink a minute, then covered the cage with my old bush shirt.

"Good-night, C.B.," he said. "See you in the morning. Good-night, Arnold. End of the line."

"End of the line!" I heard George call out. "Can't take you any farther."

And suddenly I'm swimming in snow about a hundred feet deep, but it's warm and kind of pleasant...

Chapter: 4

Well, in spite of entertaining the kids, exchanging visits with old friends and neighbours in the Square, and drinking buckets of lemon jilly water under the flame tree, on the third day I gave up predicting we'd never be ready in time and began to think we might just make it.

That day Su sent Harry for the kids in the big town car.

They were to spend the night with her, and Harry would drive them all out to Hawberry next day— the kids, Su, and Jenny. Maudy thought she wanted to stay with us and go back in the convertible, but when she saw Harry in his chauffeur's suit and then the white limo waiting in the Square, she changed her mind pretty smartly and hopped in as merry as you please.

That left Ern and me to finish the packing ready for George and Budd coming with the truck in the morning, and by mid-day everything was ready— including the sofa set. I was just drawing breath for a cheer, "Hip, hip, hurray! We're going home!" when Ern turns to me with her eyes full of tears.

"Oh, Arnold," she's blubbering, "I never thought I'd see this day. Just look at the old place. Even the geraniums..."

I put an arm around her and gave her a squeeze.

"Never mind, Ern," I said. "You can have all the geraniums you want up the Meads. And they won't have to struggle along on ten or twelve minutes of daylight once a week or so. Just wait till you see the geraniums..."

"I know, Arnold," she gulped. "But I lived here all my life. And they're going to t-tear it down! And build an arcade!"

She's bawling on my shoulder.

"Sure," I said. "I know. But you're doing the right thing, Ern... Why don't we go and look at the monks' garden now we have a minute to ourselves. You never showed me the azaleas yet..."

That seemed to work. But once we're among the flowers she starts to cry again.

"I don't know what I'm getting into, Arnold," she says. "George has been telling me things... Things I don't even begin to understand. And I don't know if I ever will. I mean, what if... I mean, Johnny was only a bad influence when I knew him, but now... The way George talks..."

"You don't have to worry, Ern," I said. "George doesn't understand it all either. No more do I."

"No, but stopping floods and I don't know what all else..."

"Ern," I said, "the way I see it now— though I agreed with George's interpretation at the time... I mean, I think it wasn't so much that Johnny stopped the flood as it was that the flood couldn't stop Johnny. Looked like he did, of course... But I think that was just the view looking up the mountain, you might say, and we ought to turn it around... Hard to explain...

"You see, Ern, when I woke up— don't know how many hours past Penner's— the bus is stopped in the middle of nowhere. Heavy snow is falling. George is just going out the door. Oomi is on the top step snapping at snowflakes. And Johnny is reaching for his coat.

I staggered out after them, shivering from being asleep and wondering what in hell I was doing there.

Once on the ground, though, I could see George and Johnny on a low mound not far off. They seemed to be looking over the terrain ahead, so I climbed up beside them and looked too.

Ern, I had to blink hard to make sure I wasn't dreaming. This great riverbed stretched ahead of us. Maybe five miles across. Gravel flats. Channels, camouflaged by snow. And here and there, when you could make out anything for the storm, these dull gray ribbons running down.

George pointed here and there. "Water," he said. "Water in the channels. Can you see it?"

"Out there?" Johnny says, pointing too.

"There and beyond. Open water. There. Not there, that's ice. The dark stuff is water. Look where it's breaking around that sandbank straight ahead."

I couldn't tell one from the other, but I took George's word for it. Anyway, the first channel was right at our feet and anybody could see it was running deep and quiet with mats of slush sliding by fast on the surface.

Looked enough of a barrier to me and I had visions of spending the night in the bus. Figured Oomi already staked out a claim on the long back seat, and didn't see much comfort in my near future. The only comfort I could think of was that winter was ending, not coming.

George seemed to think things looked pretty bad too.

"She's rising," he said. "Coming down in waves from up above and washing the fresh snow off the stream bed as she comes. Tell by the pans of slush. Sorry. No can do today."

He slid and plunged back down the side of the mound and stamped back to the bus. I came after him, but more slowly, not being used to snow then.

"I've seen The Races flooding up before," he says to me, as we're standing waiting for Johnny. "When the water's rising," he says, "there's no way across. It'll take days, maybe longer, before the fords are low enough to get the bus over. And you're sure as hell not gonna walk!"

He opened his mouth to call Johnny, but he never got any words out. Neither of us did!

And no wonder!

Johnny is standing on the mound with his head thrown back and his hair all white with snow. But the snow's falling gently around him. And behind him this pale gold light is coming through, where the sun is dissolving the layers of the storm.

George and I ran to the edge of the stream, and even I could see that a dark band of wet gravel was growing wider and wider between the gray of the water and the golden snow along the bank.

The snow was settling lightly, and everything was soft shapes and smooth gray ribbons of water running swift. Here and there this frothy, amber-coloured lace of ice covered a boulder in a stream. And the shadows under the boulders glowed like they had light of their own. I felt like I was seeing things that couldn't be really happening.

George too, I guess. He said something I didn't catch when he saw the lighted shadows and made the mountain people's blessing with his fingers in the air. While he's doing that the clouds cleared off and left the sky full of floating snowflakes sparkling in the sun.

And Johnny comes running down the mound, flapping his arms and hollering, "The water's dropping! The water's dropping!"

"I can see that," George croaks. "I see it happening. Though how you did it... Look up there. On the peaks. That's ice. It's gone cold up there and the river has dried up. If she holds, we'll get across."

"You needn't risk the bus if you think there's danger," Johnny tells him.

"There was danger," George mumbled.

Then he looked straight at Johnny. "I thought there was danger, sir," he said. "I thought there was. But I should have known better. If you'll stay up front with me and keep a lookout for soft spots, we'll go now. The first channel is dry already."

So very slowly he put the bus down the bank to the ford. She rolled a bit, but she gripped the gravel and held.

George cheered.

Johnny pounded him on the shoulder and laughed.

But being unused to it. Or cautious. Or maybe just plain scared, I kept an eye on the road.

We were running among these rocks, and dykes, and sandbanks in the river. On both sides the ice sparkled under the crowns of yellow snow.

I guess it was very beautiful. I mean, I know it was. But while I was seeing it I couldn't properly appreciate it, expecting every minute to sink into a deep hole, or break an axle, or lose the fuel tank.

Looking back, now, I know it was beautiful. And I know what I didn't know then, that it was a rare sight I was seeing. Nobody'd seen anything like it for centuries. But at the time I wasn't much interested in how beautiful it was or how long it'd been. Hardly dared breathe!

Without a word of a lie, I really believe I didn't draw a deep breath till we were across and looking back from the other side.

George pulled up over there, and Johnny was out of the bus before the wheels stopped turning, making snowballs.

I got a shower of slush down the neck and gave him a thump on the side of the head in return. George lobbed a ball at him too. But George looked like he thought he might be taking a liberty and wouldn't be too familiar all the same. Didn't know what to make of Johnny. Sometimes I think he still doesn't— judging by some of the things he's said, and some of his questions... Well, you could say Johnny made quite an impression on George at The Races.

I could say he did, easy, remembering George's face looking at me when we started hearing these sharp reports, like rifle shots, ringing out in the mountains all around us.

"Ice breaking," he says. "Time to be moving out. It isn't far to Sindabardi, as the crow flies, but there's a ridge in between and a lot of bends before we reach the top. There'll be snow on the road too, though maybe not too much the way the wind's been blowing. I reckon we can make it up by nightfall."

I looked where he was pointing, but all I saw was a solid wall of rock.

"We're going up there!?' I howled.

"It's not as bad as it looks," he says. "Three thousand feet or so out of the valley, but there's worse places, and we'll make it if we start now."

Johnny and I stood for a minute looking back at the flood that was swirling down The Races again. Rocks. Ice. Drift logs. Everything all grinding together as it came.

Johnny put a hand on my shoulder as if to say, "We're for it now, mate."

"Can't go back over it," I said. "Have to go up it... But don't be surprised if I get out and walk!"

I didn't dwell on the road out of that valley, thinking it better for Ern to find out the hard way— like I did! I skipped that part and went on up to Sindabardi as the crow flies.

Eventually— it was dark by this time, but we were over the top— the bus slowed down, stopped, and George pulled on the hand brake.

"End of the line!" he called out. "Can't take you any farther. Snow's too deep this side of the ridge. Town's just down the pass though. You won't have any trouble."

"Aren't you coming?"

"Me? No. There's a company hut just here. I'll hole up till the weather clears. No problem. Sorry to turn you out on a night like this though... You could always stay here with me, but I don't suppose..."

"We're much indebted to you," Johnny says.

"All in a day's work," George tells him, with his usual cheerful grin, though he's looking tired.

"Ask at the bakery," he says. "They won't be expecting visitors tonight, but they'll take you in. Say George sent you."

So Johnny and I put on our sheepskin coats, Oomi stretched himself down off the back seat, and the three of us left the more-or-less warm bus and waded down to Sindabardi.

Candles were lit in some of the windows and threw sparkling shapes out onto the snow. That was nice to see. But that was all there was to see. And the only sound was the shoosh of the wind lifting the snow.

George forgot to tell us, of course, that the bakery was away down at the far end of the village. But even with everything covered with snow we couldn't miss it. No other building was big enough to hold the ovens and the storage bins—except maybe the schoolhouse, and that was obvious.

Deep snow was hanging out over the eaves of the bakery, and a lot of it came thumping down onto the doorstep just as we ploughed our way almost up to it. Would have buried us alive till spring! But we were out of range and still in shadow when the door flew open and light starts pouring out of the shop. Came almost to the spot where Johnny and the cat were standing, with me coming up right behind them.

The baker was there with a broom in his hand. Not that he ever used it, when he discovered us!

He was a big fellow. Young. About my age— maybe a year or two older. And very fair. Reminded me right away of Missy so I took to him like a long-lost brother.

"Hello!" he shouts. "Anybody out there? You're just in time if you are. I was about to close up for the night."

He's peering out into the dark because he can't see farther than the light that's coming from behind him. Can't even be sure there's anybody there— till Johnny wades into sight with the cat pressing against his thigh and his hand resting on its head!!

"Hi," Johnny says. "The snow is deep and it's cold out here. Can you find us a place by your ovens for the night?"

Well, the baker's staring. But not at Johnny! For a minute he doesn't say a word. Then some kind of a light goes on in his face and this rumble comes out of his chest like he's trying to say "You're welcome" or something but he's strangling. Never heard a sound like it before or since.

In a minute though he wakes up and looks at all of us.

"You are all welcome," he says with a big smile. "Come in. It's no night to be out of doors in Sindabardi."

So we all trooped in and he closed the door behind us and helped us off with our coats. Shook them out and hung them up on wooden pegs. The cat shook his coat himself and left the floor covered with little puddles of slush and water. Funny how you remember pictures like that. Wouldn't think they'd mean anything, but they're clearer than some important things.

"George sent us," Johnny says. "We came to the edge of the village in the bus."

The baker nodded. "Of course," he said. "I am Rini Renskaya. You are more than welcome in this house. My wife has been expecting you."

That made my scalp tingle, I can tell you, Ern!

"But if she's been expecting all of you, she's been keeping it from me!" Rini says, smiling.

Johnny was watching him with that look I'd seen before— a little surprised but not much, like this was the way things ought to be and would be if the world was always run right. It took me longer to catch on.

Rini Renskaya took a candle in one hand and a basket of rolls in the other and we all started upstairs.

"This way," he says, and he leads us through the shop and the kitchen, past the ovens, and through a small doorway that opens into a dark, closed stairwell.

He went up and we followed.

At the head of the stairs he unlatched a door and stepped into a room. I noticed he ducked his head so I was prepared and didn't bang my own as we went through— always a consideration.

The room up there was warm from a big tile stove, and I felt sleepy right away. Only one candle was burning, standing on a table under a low window. I saw the table was already set for four. And there's this wonderful smell of mountain herbs coming from a soup dish and filling the room. It was like I was back with Missy and there was no winter anywhere, or ever could be.

In the middle of the room there's this dark girl standing, very quiet, with a small boy-child in her arms. She was almost like one of the shadows. Only her eyes showed clear, and something gold that she had on a chain around her neck.

"This is Noni, my wife," Rini says, and he sounds proud. "The child is Rini John."

The little boy smiled. He smelled like soap and warm clothes, and his dark curls gleamed like his mother'd just been brushing them.

Well, at that moment, Oomi pushed past us and padded into the room.

I froze. But the baker's eyes were dancing, and I could see Johnny's teeth where he was smiling wide. The mother's eyes glowed brighter too. No fear in them! And I thought she looked like we just brought her the best present she ever had in all her life.

But they were all watching the little fellow to see what he would do, and he's staring at the cat with these big blue eyes.

First he stretches out his arms. Then he looks at his mother, then back at the cat. Then he points, and whispers "Oomiskaya."

His mother laughed then and lowered him to the floor, and he stood looking up at Oomi with his hands behind his back and his stomach stuck out, big blue eyes gazing into big yellow ones.

Nobody moved, till Oomi lowers his head, nudges the baby's shoulder, very gently, and begins to purr. Hard to believe, but that's what he did. Took me a long time to get used to the fact that Oomi could purr, Ern, but the rest of them seemed to expect it. Anyway the baby did. He just flings his arms around the cat's neck and starts in crooning, "Oomiskaya. Oomiskaya."

"What's that he's saying?" Johnny whispers.

"Oomiskaya. It's the animal's name," Noni told him. "It means Lord of the High Passes."

"You and your friend are most welcome guests in this house," Rini told us. "The wisdom of our people teaches that the child who gazes deep into the eyes of Oomiskaya will climb high in safety and lead us onward when... But it is hard to imagine, isn't it! That anyone so small... One day, perhaps..."

He put a bowl of bread and soup on the floor and stood back, holding Rini John's hand, to watch their new friend drink. The food smelled good, and I was glad when I saw Noni filling more bowls and placing them on the table.

"Come," she said, "and break a fresh roll. Try one of the Jaconis."

Johnny's hand hovered over the basket. "Jaconis?" he says.

"The dark ones," the baker chuckles. "Been gone a long time, have you?"

"A long time," Johnny said. "I was not much older than your son, who shares my name. My mother took me away when I was barely five."

"And her gift?" Noni asked.

"Gift?"

"All Jaconi have a gift," Rini said.

"Oh. Well, Su is only part Jaconi," Johnny says. "I don't think she ever knew much about that side of her nature."

They looked at each other kind of puzzled.

"There are no part-Jaconi," Rini said after a minute. "One is Jaconi, or one is not. Noni, here, is Jaconi. She has a gift. You are Jaconi. You have a gift. If your mother was Jaconi, she also had a gift."

He shrugged his shoulders and smiled.

"She had, too!" Johnny exclaimed, looking at me like he suddenly understood.

"Still has," I said. "People come from all over the world to hear Su sing."

"I used to think all Jaconi were singers," Johnny said. "Black curly hair. Blue eyes. And a powerful voice."

"Is that what they think of Jaconi in the city by the rivers?" Noni asked, like she couldn't believe it.

Johnny laughed. "That's what I thought," he said. "But I didn't know much. Still don't. Some people have called me 'highalt' or 'prince.' Some think I can do magic. But you're the first Jaconi I've actually met. Besides myself. And Su."

"Not me," the baker said quickly. "Just Noni. And maybe Rini John."

"Maybe?" Johnny asked. "Is there a doubt?"

Noni smiled and looked at her child kneeling beside the cat, crooning softly and listening to him purr.

"He likes me, Mama," he said. "Listen to him sing."

"Many people believe that the colouring makes us Jaconi," Noni said. "Just as many suppose that Rini is strong to lead because his hair is flaxen and his eyes are gray. They think the fair hair makes him ebrit, but that is the same as saying that the sun comes up in the morning because he has a yellow face. Rini may be descended from the Grand Ebrits, as they say, but he is ebrit, guardian, because he is wise and gentle... far-seeing... prudent... fair..."

"I make good bread too," Rini chuckled.

He did, too, and whoever made the soup made good soup. I stuffed myself.

After the soup, Rini brought us mugs of a sweet, hot drink, like all the honey of summer poured into each cup.

"Push your chair back and be comfortable," he said to me. "Those two will talk all night, but there's no need for us to sit bolt upright at the table. We'll stay till the child sleeps. Then I'll take him to his crib and you can stretch out beside the stove. Rest now. Drink your tea."

So I drank my tea and my eyelids drooped. I was warm and comfortable. Missy came and went in my head, beautiful and happy. But I was aware of everything in the room too, and none of it surprised me. I mean, even with my eyes closed I saw the baby cuddle up with his head against Oomi's side and fall asleep; saw the two dark heads leaning together across the table, and the medallions flashing.

And nothing surprised me. Because I was just looking on, I think. Just being there; not in it. Maybe that's why I remember it all so clear.

"...pain," I heard Noni say.

Johnny shuddered.

"And grief... I'll help you if I can."

"Who am I?" Johnny whispered.

She drew back, like she was surprised again. "You fear your gift," she said. "The healing of the burns..."

"They thought I did that."

"And the crossing of the fords."

"I didn't do that!"

She smiled.

"No!"

"Not since the greatfathers of old have we seen such deeds," she said. "But your gift is great."

"No!" Johnny shouted.

"I felt the sudden cold," she said, "and I saw the fords laid bare for you to cross."

"You must have done it then."

She shook her head.

She looked sad.

"I have no such gift," she said. "I see and hear lives, a little. I sense the world turning, sometimes. I know hearts and that way help, if anyone is willing. But I do not move mountains... Or halt floods."

"But you know things," Johnny's pleading. "And you understand. You must. I know nothing. Help me."

"You can see too," she said. "Look away to the stars and do not be afraid. There is much that I, too, would learn."

"A shadowy man," Johnny whispers. "I used to meet him sometimes, but not now. Did I dream him? 'A shadowy man in shadowy clothes, With a kitten's scratch at the end of his nose. Old and weak but full of power, An old man in a stone tower?"

"Oh, that I knew," Noni says, and sighs.

And there was something in her voice that I can only say was like when you feel all sole alone in the world.

In that warm room smelling of drying herbs. With her baby asleep at her feet. And Rini there, proud to bursting of them both. On this special night, she's lonely. I almost cried.

"Much has been forgotten, and much of the ancient wisdom has been lost," she said. "Some of that little song is not... not just as it used to be... The last line, certainly... I wish I had more to give you."

"I thought, when I found Jaconi..."

Her eyes filled with tears. "No," she said.

Then she smiled. "I have heard of your shadowy man," she said, "but he has not come my way. Some say he has been abroad on the flat rivers these many years. In the mountains he is called Yaanskaya."

The cat opened his eyes and his tail twitched.

"Lord of Humankind," she said. "Perhaps only a children's tale... Sindabardi is only a waymark on your journey. You must go farther."

Johnny leaned toward her again. "Where is Medalsring?" he said.

"High. Very high in the great range."

The medallion around his neck shot fire. "Then it exists?" he says. "You know it? What is it like?"

"No, no, Jaconi," Noni said. "You hope too much. I cannot see Medalsring, for there is no-one there. Legend says it was a tall fortress of white stone that sheltered its people on the high crags, where music was heard all the day long, and men did not suffer pain or hunger... But it is empty now."

"Nobody goes there?" Johnny whispered.

"No-one knows the way," she said. "Though, perhaps, now that Oomiskaya has come, my son will lead us when he has grown tall and strong."

"The child will follow me," Johnny said. "The prophecy has already been fulfilled."

Noni's eyes widened. "Long, straight shadows," she murmured. "And a

child's fingers stretching toward a golden muzzle marked with black... Love...
Patience. Fear!"

"My mother was afraid," he said.

"Beware the rivers of the south," Noni whispered.

The rivers of the south.

Delta rivers.

Ern, I was rushing down the marshes on the barging streams. Heard grass
rustling, barges creaking. Watched a heron slat away across a slough on those
tanbark wings they have. Saw the City rise from the mud. Hovered over Red
Dragon Square, Red Andy's, squiggy buns, a pink geranium.

But...

"Jenny," Johnny groaned.

"Jenny," Noni echoed. "Gentleness and faith."

And, Ern, I wished I'd thought of that myself, because that was exactly
what Jenny was.

"Jenny," Johnny whispered again, through his hands.

"Jenny is brightness of morning where sun burns," Noni said. "She is
starfire at evening... Freedom of small mice that fly in moonlight... Flower...
Child... Boy..."

"She needed me and I couldn't help her!" Johnny cried.

And everything rushed together again— the light over the door, Farmer's
voice snarling, the stone the kid threw, the blood on Farmer's face, his dog bleeding
in the dust, the roses shrivelling... And the baby, whimpering, dying in his
mother's arms.

"So now you know," Johnny sobs. "I'm no miracle-worker. I'm a fraud.
Old Marion sent me to keep the yellow snow. To keep the yellow snow on that
bloody river down below, for God's sake! Arnold was right. We should have gone
back to Wooji and made a mint of money mining blue-rock. Who the hell do I
think I am!"

But Noni stayed very still.

And Johnny got up and stood by the window looking out into the sky where the stars were coming out as the storm cleared. Every one of his muscles was cramped, tight to trembling.

But after awhile he got hold of himself and sat down again. "This hasn't happened for a long time," he says. "Forgive me, Noni. I'm sorry."

"Not since you slept under the aspens of Eavenen," she told him. "Where the golden leaves float on the Mirror Pool."

"Eavenen of the gentle shades'? And not a dream?"

"Not a dream."

"And afterward?"

"It is impossible... afterward..."

Ern, I saw us leaving Canalhead all over again.

Johnny picked up his pack, and it was just like the day it happened. I didn't think I could do it then, and I didn't think I could do it when I lived it over. Standing on Mrs. Presking's front verandah with Missy, I didn't think I could do it.

I looked south over the marshes and my mind stood on the bank of the canal at Hawberry. I heard the clank of barge cable. My back ached again from the paddle, just like it did before. I saw Missy smile at the kitchen table; heard her say, "Louisa was my sister."

I got all mixed up, Ern, and saw myself walking into Red Dragon Square with a fair-haired wife and son. After awhile nobody would remember Cally wasn't mine, ours. I bought a flower shop, painted the old house, pruned the flame tree...

But just then a blue and purple crankybird flew in off the south dyke and shrieked, skimming the town. One of the mountain breed on a course for the hills, and I said, "Promise you won't try to get down to the City by the barges?"

"I won't," Missy promised.

Then she threw her arms around me. "I won't," she said. "I've got a job and a home here now."

Cally came to hug me too, but he had to settle for hugging us both together and wait his turn. I wasn't about to let Missy go, not when she started it.

I saw her head shining against the hills and I knew I could never let the Red Dragon breathe on her. I'd find a home. But it would have to be somewhere in country I didn't know yet. Somewhere I had to go alone first.

I think I would have told her then, in words, but the whole town came to see us off, and Cally and Buster were beside themselves with excitement.

"You still don't have to come, you know," Johnny said, close to my ear.

"I think I do," I told him.

And I started to sing, making up the words as I went, "Can't go down again, have to go up again. Can't stay put here, have to stay put there..."

Johnny joined in. "Can't go under it, have to go over it. Can't go over it, have to go around it. Can't go..."

Pretty soon everybody in Canalhead was singing us off. Kids and dogs ran after us. All the shop-keepers came to their doors and hollered good-bye. The baker ran out with a bag of fresh rolls. Even the manager of The Marshlands stood on the verandah and waved, and I almost believe it wasn't only because he knew by then Johnny was Su Doyle's son and had a bankroll that would choke a horse.

We stopped at the bridge over the stream for the last hugs.

All the people squinted in the early light.

They reached for our hands, pounded our shoulders, kissed our cheeks.

We hugged Cally again and again, and told Buster, "Down, fellah," again and again.

We hugged Mrs. Presking, the banker's wife, the baker's wife, everybody's wife, mother, and grandmother.

Johnny hugged Missy and said something to her that I didn't hear.

I hugged Missy.

She kissed me.

I kissed her.

I hugged her again...

And so, Ern, we went northeast into a wooded valley that passies tell us leads to a deep cleft in the hills. The river chatters over loose stones. Beside the river, the road runs. Wild flowers bloom after the rains. Insects hum. A few birds chirp and hop around.

Days go by, and we have only the valley and ourselves for company. Travelling north by east. Measuring the road by foot-falls.

Tired-looking men with heavy packs and women carrying children passed us sometimes, hurrying south. They'd turn when they left us behind to look back at the two crazymen striding north, and we'd wave to them.

The leaves on the aspens along the river turn to gold and shine among the evergreens on the slopes.

And always the blue sky.

Always the sky...

After a long time... After a long time, one day we came to a stream running down from a valley high above. It crossed the road in this shallow wash and spilt into the river over a lip of rock.

The sun shone.

Birds chirped.

The stream leapt down the hillside among the aspen trees with their golden leaves.

And just as if we knew what we were doing, we left the road and began to climb... race to pool... pool to fall.. fall to race...

In the warm hours of the afternoon we came to a small, still pool reflecting the blue of the sky and the gold of the trees. A few yellow leaves floated on the water.

On the far side of the pool, a pair of river otters stopped playing and watched us. Black. Sleek little felllows. Bright-eyed. I stretched out a hand toward them and they slid into the water like beams of light going out.

We dropped our packs and waited.

In a moment they broke the surface again, closer to us, watching.

We sat against the trees, keeping still.

They watched.

We didn't move.

Then one of them nudged the other, and they both flipped over and disappeared... without a ripple.

But in a split-second they were back, bursting through the mirror together. And one of them was wearing this leaf on its head, like a golden hat!

It darts up a lip of the rock where this waterfall is coming down. It drops the leaf back in. And it's under that leaf before it touches the water! Truth, Ern! Before it touches the water.

"Oiled shadows!" Johnny whispered.

We watched them play in the sun. Watched the leaves drifting down one by one. Looked at each other. And slid in after them.

The pool held us, and the otters played in the currents we made. We floated out of the world and played with them.

All in the afternoon.

All in the afternoon, Ern.

But when the sun disappeared behind a bluff and a cool breeze flowed down the valley, we pulled out of the pool and rested, feeling good, contented, drying in the open air, happy.

Pretty soon darkness settled in.

And just before full dark, these three small deer came to drink and pass on up the gully. I saw them like you see shadows, but I heard their hooves on the path.

For a long time that night I sat with my back against an old aspen.

Johnny sat by the water, staring into the mirror.

When the moon came up, the golden leaves turned silver. Still, now and then, one of them floated down.

After awhile...

After...

Who knows?

My eyelids closed.

I slept... woke...

Johnny was still sitting by the pool, and the moon still reflected off the mirror, but the glade was filled with pain. I would have helped him, but I drifted off again...

Woke...

This time two shadows sat by the pool. One held her long hair back from the water.

"No," I told myself. "Illusion. Dreaming."

But after that... peace... and deep sleep... and in the morning... joyful.

It was like that again the night we spent in Sindabardi, but in the morning Rini had fresh buns baked, and we stood at the counter down in the bakery and stuffed ourselves with them while we watched snow steam on the doorstep and icicles drip from under the eaves...

I stopped talking for a minute, then, and let myself come back from the Mirror Pool and the snow on the doorstep.

There was a quiet humming in the monks' garden, and the flowers shimmered under the weight of bees. I almost lost myself again in a white blossom that opened up to a narrow beam of sunlight and showed a pale flush of pink...

But Ern, after a minute, put her hand over mine and whispered, "Go on, Arnold. You'd better. I need to know it all."

I drew a deep breath...

Ern," I said, "you've never seen anything like it, and I hadn't either at the time. The whole world was white to the peaks and clear blue beyond, with the sun blazing in the sky, holding it all together.

With our hoods thrown back and our eyes narrowed against the light, we followed the baker out of the village onto this flat expanse of alpine meadow, deep in snow, that stretched away to a great mass of rock that backed the village.

Rini flapped a mitten toward the mountain and told us, "Sindabardi. Same as the village... You can stay here with us!" Sounded good to me, on snowshoes for the first time in my life, and pulling a loaded toboggan behind.

He pointed to the far side.

"There's a notch over there," he said. "Can you see it? We'll make for that. It's the only way into the heart of the massif."

It looked a long way to me.

"You needn't go till spring," he said again, like he could read thoughts too.

Johnny looked away to the notch in the rock and said nothing.

"You could go up with the sheep," Rini said. "The high meadows are friendly places in summer, but now... You'll have to shelter in the herders' huts."

"We'll be all right," Johnny said then.

Rini squinted at him and shook his head.

"I reckon," he said. "But take care. Find some sort of shelter before night comes on. These mountains can be very cold when the air cools on the heights and sinks down the gullies. And never trust a stream bed. There can be sun on top, and if the ice lets go..."

He was looking at Johnny, but I had a feeling these practical instructions were really aimed at me and I took them all in.

"I'll go as far as the notch with you," he said. "I'd go farther, but this time of year my place is with my people."

Ern, that notch led out of a steep ravine that fell into a valley far below and ran down and away from Sindabardi, below and behind the town. You'll see when we get there.

Rini led us along the edge of the ridge where it dropped away. The upward course was always out of sight around a shoulder of the mountain, but I could see snow blowing in light clouds up there, where a wind was lifting the powder surface of the field. It didn't look good to me. But what did I know! Johnny was the mountain man.

Near the notch Rini stopped and waited for us to come up with him.

"There's the entrance," he said. "The wind's blowing hard in there. I've been watching it for an hour or so, and it's going to be very cold. Nobody would think less of you if you came back with me."

"Thanks," Johnny said, "but I've come this far. Arnold, of course..."

I shook my head.

Rini nodded, but he hesitated before he spoke again.

"Have you thought?" he said then. "Have you thought? Medalsring may not be there."

"I've thought," Johnny replied, "and it doesn't seem to matter."

It was the first time I thought though, and it gave me a turn. Not that I ever had any choice either, really. But you like to think you're in charge.

Well, that afternoon it didn't take me long to figure out I wasn't in charge of much of anything. Dark was already gathering in the ravine. All the new snow had been swept out by the wind, and the rocks were black and bare. The air roared after the silence of the snowfield, and glittering falls of ice snapped as they cooled and tightened.

Rini drew me close under the cliff where we could hear a little better.

"The first hut is not far up," he shouted. "Just past the turning. By that blue fall. Can you see that?"

I nodded.

"Follow the natural path upward," he said. "Don't cross the stream. And don't, ever, go down to find an easier way up somewhere else. Remember that!"

I signalled that I understood.

"It will be very cold in there, but you'll make it," he shouted, and grasped my hand.

I gave him a clout on the shoulder. Then, pulling the hood of my coat close around my face, I went in.

The wind shrieked down the canyon.

Johnny was already climbing, bent almost double, pulling his toboggan after him.

My thighs burned. My chest couldn't get enough of that high, thin air. But Johnny was well ahead, allowing for no weakness, and I plunged on...

I remember only the pain now, but I know that before full dark we reached a depression in bedrock, carpeted with dry grass, where a hut sheltered against the far wall.

The door opened at a push from Johnny's shoulder and we fell into the room. I could hardly stand. But the wind didn't follow us in, and we left the door open and eased off our packs. The light from the doorway showed us a hearth already laid with dry grass and twigs. More fuel was piled in a corner. Clean animal skins hung over lines. And there was ice in a covered crock.

Pretty soon I was feeling better. Ate a little. And stretched out on a pile of skins and slept.

In the night I woke. The door was open, and by starlight I saw Johnny sitting on the doorstep.

"What are you doing?" I croaked, but he didn't hear me.

I got up and tried to get him to come back and shut the door.

"No. The mountain people are coming," he said. "They're cold. I can see them shivering under their winter clothes. Watch. You'll see their cloaks flapping around them."

"No," I said. "There's nobody there."

"Yes," Johnny said. "Sometimes they glance this way, but they never stop to speak."

"Come back to the fire," I told him, but he started up and called out to somebody.

"What was that about?" I asked, trying to sound normal.

"A dark-haired girl and a small child, hand in hand," he said. "For a minute I thought it was Su and Johnny."

I got him back into the hut and he fell into a deep sleep. Not me, though. I was still awake a long time later when Oomi pushed open the door and crept up to the warm hearth stones.

"Lord love us," I thought. "Between the two of them, it's a good thing I'm along."

Little did I know!

Very little did I know!

Snow fell.

The wind howled.

More snow fell.

But day by day we climbed up that ravine, stumbling in our winter clothes, dragging the loaded toboggans.

Cloud covered the mountain all the time, but we kept on going— till one day the gully ended in this little, black, frozen tarn lying under an overhang of rock and ice that closed the way ahead.

End of the line.

We stayed in a hut at the base of the ice-fall, and waited.

More snow fell.

The cloud never lifted.

Every morning we walked to the fall and Johnny said, "Tomorrow." And every evening he studied the rock and ice and said again, "Tomorrow."

One morning, when we had been there awhile— I don't know how long— and the mist was as thick as ever, I knocked my head on the door frame coming out, again! And something snapped. I stood in the middle of that black, frozen, God-forsaken little tarn and howled.

"What in hell are we doing here!?" I roared. "Down below, the sun is shining. Up above, there's sun! And warm feet, for God's sake! And dry clothes! Up there, light's flowing up and down the rocks like it thinks cloud is something you play with! But us! What in hell are we doing here!?"

Almost before the words were out of my mouth I was sorry I said them, because Johnny was looking at me with something in his face that scared me.

"No!" I started to say, but he went straight to the place where the stream came down, sprang onto a narrow ledge, and plunged into the mist.

He was gone before I knew it.

I hollered for him to come back. I yelled at him and swore. Most of that day I stamped around below the fall getting madder and madder and more and more terrified.

At last I gave it up and went back to the hut.

"To hell with you!" I roared.

Then I turned right around and went in after him— into that cloud of frozen fog hanging on the rocks.

No up or down.

Not even before and after.

Just me.

And cold.

And pain...

Till these rainbow colours and opal ghosts started coming and going.

Light flashed from shifting centres.

The mist thinned.

I brushed aside the last streamers— and I was back on the black tarn again! By the shepherds' hut.

"Damn this bloody mountain!" I roared.

But no.

It wasn't.

Not the place I left.

"Another bloody cirque," I yelled. "Another one! Another bloody little cirque. And Johnny's gone on up. Oh, God!"

Thin cloud came down again and hid the way, so I sat on my coat on a ledge of rock and let the misty sun bake the aches out of my back and shoulders.

After awhile Oomi came and rubbed his nose against my leg, before he leapt into the cloud and disappeared too.

"Can't even trust the bloody cat," I muttered, but I followed him.

Slipped and fell.

Must have hit my head.

Came to, sore and bleeding from the temple, wedged between two rocks. And Oomi's standing over me and whining.

My coat was gone.

"All right, Oomi," I said. "I'm awake now. Let's go."

After awhile— I don't know how long— I clawed my way onto a wet ledge that was hard to grip. Pulled myself up— and there's Johnny's coat caught on a spur of rock. .

That scared me, I can tell you, Ern, but I couldn't find blood on it anywhere.

Noticed the air felt warmer up there though; water was trickling over the rocks.

Went on.

Slipped a lot.

Bled.

Burned.

Sweat and blood ran into my eyes and blurred my vision, but there was no place to stop, so I kept on till a long while later— I think it was— till I shook my head to clear my sight, and just after I opened my eyes again, this bright thing, not ice, metallic, glittering, came sliding down the gully. Grabbed it and stuffed it in my pocket.

More than my eyesight needed clearing by this time. Couldn't seem to think. Sat on a rock. Sat in a puddle— didn't see any reason not to.

My mind wandered.

Ears roared.

I thought thunder was shaking the mountain. And almost too late I threw myself under this overhang just as a wall of water, rock, and ice poured over me!

The mountain shook like it was in an earthquake.

Ice and rock crashed down the gully.

Huge blocks of the mountain shattered, and sharp bits flew at my face and hands.

Brown water squirted right out of the rock, it seemed, in thin streams, and I thought it was my blood squirting from my cuts. Didn't know where it was going. Far as I could see I was in some black hole somewhere that was missing top and sides. "Johnny!" I yelled.

Over, and over, and over. Round, and round, and round. "Johnny! Oh, God! Johnny!" I yelled.

I was sure I was shrinking.

I shrivelled right up and turned black. Thought I was no more than this little, dry kernel, like a seed caught in a crack in the rock.

"God," I howled.

But the rocks went on splitting forever. Ice blocks ground together as they fell. And the mountain went on shaking.

Sometimes I hung on by my fingernails— my ledge kept lurching and tilting.

Mud oozed over my hands, onto my face, into my mouth.

"Get off of me!" I yelled.

The mountain lurched again.

I thought I was gone.

"God!" I yelled.

But the mud slid off me and dribbled into the abyss.

And then— water was still thundering into the valley, but I began to see peaks all around me. Saw them through mist, in and out, but clear... graceful... lovely... endless. Johnny's infinity, I guess... Must have been still dizzy from the pounding, but it sure was beautiful.

I just laid there and watched, looking out. Didn't dare look down. Sat with my knees pulled up under my chin and my arms wrapped around them. Just sat on what was left of my ledge being thankful, till the water passed.

After awhile Oomi showed up and I wasn't so scared with company. Looked around at the ravine gleaming with water, and out— away out— to the universe unrolling before me. Everything seemed to be sparkling. Shining and ordered. Circles turning in these pure, unbroken patterns.

And all of a sudden I felt real happy, like it was for the first time in my life.

"You know something, Oomi?" I said. "There are no screams under the gargoyles. There's no wind on the mountain. I just found out."

He looked like he knew that all along, but he purred and nudged my shoulder.

"Here!" I hollered. "Do you want to push me off? I wouldn't stop till I shot out the bottom into our little tarn. And I'm warning you, I'll take you with me!"

By then the avalanche is ending in this trickle of ice and water, and the moon is rising pale over the peaks in the east. I stood up and stretched my muscles, one by one, testing my strength, making sure everything was working— making sure I was ready for the mountain.

Then, Ern, slowly at first, but growing stronger as I went, I finished the climb.

Lumps of ice as big as houses were down here and there. Huge trees and rocks from the slopes lay across the path. But I went on, along these "beautiful, orderly, precise, and joyous lines and circles of creation"— Johnny's words, not mine....

After awhile, the moon slid behind a spur, but the stars were still bright. And soon, it seemed to me, a line of light appeared over the rim of the cliffs and a new day started down into the ravine.

Near the top I caught up with Oomi. He was sliding down a frozen channel on his haunches. Perfectly dignified. Having the time of his life! And I burst out laughing.

The noise I made disturbed what I thought was icicles hanging to the rim along the line of daylight, but they broke off and rose into the air on wings. Watched them swing upward toward the day. Then I went after them.

But there's this thin veil of water splashing over the last lip, the last step that's not for me— not yet. And I was drying my hands on my pants for the twenty-fifth time, ready to try again, when somebody leans over and says, "What took you so long? Oomi's been up and down a dozen times."

I nearly fell off the mountain! But I grabbed the hand he reached down to me and bounded up...

"Welcome to Medalsring," he said.

We were standing at the edge of this shallow pool, Ern, that filled the last cirque in the chain. Buttercups and daisies were swaying in a light breeze. The perfume of roses came from among the rocks. And meadow land stretched beyond.

Not far off, sheep were grazing on new spring grass. And to one side, six or seven small stone houses straggled up a cliff. For the rest, Ern, this blue-green, blue-white, blue-fresh valley opened out, full of sun and rain, and birds and flowers, and backed by another mighty range in the distance.

"Glad you could make it," Johnny said. "The road is finished."

I looked back and there it was, looping away down the canyon. Past the ice falls. Past the ledge where the avalanche flowed over me. Bridging the gap where I found the medallion. Past our black tarn, shining now with open water. And away on, down the gully track, into the far, far distance.

I reached into my pocket. "I think this is yours," I said.

He smiled, took the medallion, and hung it around my neck. "Yours now, Jaconi," he said.

Chapter: 5

So there I was, on time, pulling out of Hawberry with my caravan. Felt like old Jacon Jaconi himself.

George left first with some of the passengers and the hand baggage in the van. I followed in Johnny's convertible with a full load of passengers— of the younger variety. And Budd brought up the rear in the truck.

At the bridge, Budd made George and me come back and lead him. Then he very gingerly put the truck across.

"Trucker's nightmare, them bridges are," he said, when we were all over. "No underpinnings to speak of. All the strength in the timbers. No guard rails. And slippery! First sign of wet weather, look out! I give that one six months and she'll be out again."

I wondered a bit about that.

No trouble on the marshes, though. Still dry. We crossed in three days, travelling by daylight and camping nights in huts the truckers used. Hadn't been much business for a couple of years, but the huts were sound and sheltered us from the night wind that was still cold.

The van turned out to be as sweet as George claimed. The truck didn't sink in soft ground as half of Hawberry predicted. And everybody stayed excited and happy.

The Athertons opened up like apricot blossoms. The nearer we got to the hills, the better they looked.

George and I, of course, we were glad to be going home.

Even Su took to the road like she was gypsy born. Didn't show any regrets, though she knew as well as anybody that none of us would ever be coming back.

Jenny began to brown up and smile more. She was still quiet, but she was happy to be getting nearer to Johnny every day, and her eyes shone when I talked to her about him.

And Ern. Well, Ern was the biggest surprise of all! You'd think she'd been camping out all her life. Learned everything she could. Never stopped putting the questions to Alice. Hopped out every chance she got to gather plants and flowers. And more often than not, I noticed, when we got going for the day, she was in the little jump seat up the front of the van, beside George.

We were all happy and excited, but I was suffering from a particular kind of nervousness that got worse the closer we came to the Canalhead road junction. Thought it didn't show at the time. Figured I could hide it in among the general high spirits. Me! With Ern around!

So on the fifth evening, the night we reached the turnoff, I said, casual as I could manage, "Day off tomorrow, folks. I have to go over to Canalhead. May be gone a day or two, so you can stretch your legs."

Sitting by the campfire under the stars, I pictured them all scurrying off like ants in all directions— Ern dragging George somewhere to look for plants, Alice picking berries, Budd studying all the scrubby little trees that grew on the slopes, Jack exercising Cranky....

It was all in aid of keeping my mind off the next day or two, of course— and of course it didn't work. My stomach churned and my head spun round and round.

But the time came, and at last, two years and six months late, I drove the convertible into Canalhead by the track over the foothills, and parked by Mrs. Presking's hen-run fence.

Chickens were still there. Nobody else though. Thought the place was deserted till Mrs. P peeked through the lace curtains to see who was parking on her property and nearly blew a gasket. You'd think I'd been dead and come back to life to see her gallop through the back door and across the yard!

"They're not here!" she hollers.

I nearly passed out on the spot.

"Cally's in school," she pants. "Missy's working. And the dog, he's about his business somewhere. Why didn't you let us know!?"

"Mrs. P," I howled. "You almost gave me heart failure, hollering 'They're not here.' Think what you're saying, woman!"

"And serve you right," she hoots. "Staying away all these years."

"Only two and a half."

"Only two and a half!" she hollers. "Fine for you young fellows. But for a girl like Missy? What were you thinking of!? You need to drop down on your knees right here and now and thank the Almighty she's even still in town, let alone still waiting for you. For what she sees in you, I'll never know, and her with her chances. Where's the other one?"

She looked past my shoulder the way they all did.

"He isn't here," I said. "He's back in the hills. I came down to see to a few things— and find Missy."

"Well, she'll be leaving the bakery just about now," Mrs. P hoots, "so you better get yourself on up the square and catch her."

I moved fast and was just in time, rounding the Business Bank, to see her coming out and turning to make sure the bakery screen door was shut before she started down the street.

Seeing her, I stopped. It was like I was rooted right there, like my eyes were the only part of me that still worked.

There she was. My Missy. Tall. Long pale braid over her shoulder. Brown from the sun. But she looked tired. Sort of dragged her feet as she came toward me.

If only my legs would have moved, I'd have caught her up and carried her home in my arms. But as things were, all I could do was promise myself I'd look after her better from now on.

Part way along she hitched up a linen sling she had across her shoulder, but still she didn't look up.

Eyes on the ground.

Past the hardware store, scuffling along in the dust. Brushing her hair back with her hand.

Looking up.

She sees me!

For a minute she doesn't move. Then her shoulders straighten, the spring comes back in her step. And she smiles. And keeps on smiling.

She walked right up to me looking straight at me. Never even blinked till she was so close her eyes refused to stay open any longer. All along the square she looked at me, and never once glanced past my shoulder.

"Can you be ready to leave tomorrow?" I muttered, as soon as I could speak.

"Yes," she said.

After that there was laughing and hugging, hand shaking and back slapping. But what came first, or who started it, I'll never know.

Cally came home from school talking. Most of it went in one ear and out the other, but the gist was that a trip into the mountains would be just what he'd like but would he have to go to school when he got there?

"You'll like this school," I told him. "The teacher is real pretty."

"Don't care what she looks like," he said. "Is she afraid of caterpillars? Old Ms. Willoughby screeches every time she sees one."

"Crawling in her hair?" I suggested, and he grinned.

Buster remembered me enthusiastically. He was full of burrs, as usual, and most of them rubbed off on me.

Mrs P laughed and cried, ran in and out, seemed to be there when I didn't want her and gone when I did.

Before long it was clear I'd have to be in four or five places at once, but after the past couple of weeks I was getting used to that and didn't mind.

Never knew the hour and couldn't quite catch on when Cally and Buster showed signs of being hungry. Eat? Eat? What did they mean?

While I was trying to come to grips with that idea, Mrs. P came rushing into the house with the baker's wife and Ms. Willoughby from the school.

"Arnold," they hooted, everybody talking at once, "you'll have to go right up to The Marshlands and have a word with that manager."

"Why? On this of all days? We were never particular friends."

"He has rented the ballroom to a party from out of town!" Ms. Willoughby announced.

"Oh, my stars!" Mrs. bakery yodelled at that moment. "He'll never remember to take the cake out of the oven." She galloped away followed by slamming screen doors, and I heard her whooping all the way up the square.

"What do you want with the ballroom, ladies?" I said cautiously. I had a sneaking suspicion and a Lord-help-me! feeling in the pit of my stomach.

"Dancing!" Mrs. Presking snapped. "What did you think we wanted it for? Get on up there and engage the room for this evening. Without fail."

No use arguing. So with Cally and Buster running circles around me and getting under my feet, I strode up the square, up the steps of the hotel— and ran smack into the manager just coming through the door.

"Well, well, well!" he says, with this big grin. "So we've come back, have we? Never expected it. You're a brave man— for a foolish one! Leaving that sweet little girl breaking her heart down here in Canalhead. What were you thinking of? If you hadn't come back this year, I'd have moved in there myself."

If I hadn't felt more like punching him out, I would've had to smile. Missy could look right over this little guy's head and down the other side, even though he wore his hair puffed up as high as he could.

"Seems we need your ballroom for this evening," I said, ignoring his bleats.

"Grieve," he says, reaching up to my shoulder and whispering like we were old pals. "Mate," he says, "it can't be done. And so I told Mrs. Presking and the other ladies. A party from out of town came in not half an hour ago and took the room for dinner and the rest of the evening. Everything of the best. No expense spared. Flowers. Wine. Pastries."

"Give them some other room," I said.

"Couldn't do it, Arnold," he says. "Like to help you, seeing you're an old friend and it's the ladies of the town asking, but..."

"Loaded are they? This party from out of town?"

"I should say so," he murmured. "The lady in charge, I am sure even on slight acquaintance, is very well-heeled indeed. Not to be denied."

Just then I hear this full, carrying, female voice. It's raised— imperiously, I think the word is. And it's saying, "Where is that disappearing young man who calls himself manager of this hostelry? Young man? Manager? Where are you?"

The disappearing little manager spins in place for a second, like he's trying to decide whether to answer her or run for his life, but I put him firmly behind me and start down the corridor for the ballroom.

"Su!" I bellow.

"Arnold?" she says sweetly. "You're not supposed to be here!"

Then she rounds on the manager who's half hidden behind me. "About those potted palms," she says.

They were all there— George and Budd, grinning ear to ear. Ern and Alice lugging in flowers from the little conservatory where they kept petunias and geraniums over the winter. Jenny and Maudy stringing fairy lights. The boys helping the porter set up tables and chairs. Maids. Bell-boys. Even Cranky, standing on a perch in a gilded cage and squawking at the top of his lungs.

"We're using his feathers for our colour scheme," Ern tells me.

"What in hell are you doing here?" I roared. "I left you lot back on the road and expected you to stay there!"

"What!? And leave you to get married all by yourself!?" she howled.

"How do you know I'm getting married!" I yelled. "Maybe I only came over here to..."

"Nonsense!" Su says. "We are not children, though you sometimes appear to think so. Of course you're getting married. Aren't you?"

"Of course he is," Mrs. Presking puts in, pushing forward out of the mob that's already collected by the door and growing every minute. Even Mrs. bakery was there, bobbing up and down at the back, no doubt late because of taking the cake out of the oven.

"Of course he's getting married," Mrs. P says. "If he thinks he can sneak Missy away from her friends before he takes his vows, he's got another think coming! And who might you be?"

"I," says Su— and means it— "am as close as Arnold comes to having a mother. Who are you?"

"I," says Mrs. P, "can say the same for Missy."

"Then we have work to do," Su says, all smiles and linking her arm in Mrs. P's. "First you can introduce me to the baker."

"Here I am!" Mrs. the-baker's-wife yodels, and the knot of people in the doorway breaks up to let her through.

I escaped down the square to find Missy. Only Buster seemed to notice I was going, and he couldn't make up his mind whether to stick with me or hang around the party, experience having taught him that parties and food go together, whereas with me—maybe yes, maybe no.

Missy was upstairs in her room packing.

"They're planning a big shindig," I yelled up the stairs. "Su and Ern and the whole gang are over here, and Mrs. P and the others..."

She looked down over the banister and smiled. "I was afraid of that," she told me.

"Missy..." I said.

Then I took the stairs three or four at a time and got a good grip on her before I finished. "Missy, they're going to make you marry me before they'll let you go."

She pulled away far enough to look me in the eyes. "Do you want to, Arnold?" she whispered.

"Me!" I howled.

Then I grinned, just before I kissed her.

"Just watch me," I said.

I remember clearly only one other moment before Smallest Granddaughter was climbing all over me, making fast friends with Maudy, and keeping a cautious eye on Cranky all at the same time.

It was when we crossed the wash where the stream came down that flowed out of the Mirror Pool. I called a halt and took Jenny by the hand. She was strong then and climbed easily up the gully, touching stones and flowers as she went, noticing all the colours, listening to the birds, dipping her fingers in the water.

By the pool she knelt a long time. Finally the old Jenny we knew up to Wooji looked up and smiled.

As I waited for her, I watched the others gathering behind her, not making a sound, just being there, happy.

Missy came and settled in the circle of my arm.

Then Su began to sing...

Photo by Flewwelling

ABOUT THE AUTHOR

Yvonne Wilson has been teacher, editor, and writer. In Canada she has lived and worked in Quebec and British Columbia as well as in her native New Brunswick. She has also lived and worked in Australia and New Zealand. Since leaving the University of New Brunswick Saint John, where she helped establish the writing lab, she has been giving courses for the New Brunswick Consortium of Writers and editing fiction manuscripts for Consortium members. Red Dragon Square is her second novel.